77TH ANNUAL Writer's Digest Writing Competition

COLLECTION

The Grand-Prize and First-Place Manuscripts in Each Category of the 77th Annual *Writer's Digest* Writing Competition

90069 • *Writer's Digest* • 4700 East Galbraith Road • Cincinnati, OH 45236

INTRODUCTION

The editors of *Writer's Digest* are pleased to share with you the winning entries in each category of the 77th Annual *Writer's Digest* Writing Competition, along with the Grand Prize-winning stage play, *The Mistress of Wholesome*, by Jacob M. Appel.

A special thanks goes to our esteemed panel of judges:

• Judge **Hollis Gillespie** (Memoirs/Personal Essay) is a syndicated humor columnist, NPR commentator and guest on *The Tonight Show with Jay Leno*. Her third book, *Trailer Trashed: My Dubious Efforts Toward Upward Mobility* (Globe-Pequot) was just released. Her previous two books have been optioned for television and are currently in pre-production. Her popular memoir-writing seminar, titled "The Shocking Real-Life Memoir-Publishing Seminar" (hollisgillespie.com/seminar.htm), is currently on tour throughout the Southeast.

• Judge **JA Konrath** (Genre Short Story) is the author of the Lt. Jack Daniels thrillers, the latest of which is *Fuzzy Navel*. His books have been published in ten languages, and he's sold more than 60 stories and articles since 2004. Visit him at JAKonrath.com.

• Judge **Debby Mayne** (Mainstream/Literary Short Story)—writer, teacher and editor—has been an author of fiction and nonfiction for nearly 20 years. Upcoming book releases include *Georgia Weddings* in April 2009, *Love Finds You in Treasure Island, Florida*, in June 2009, and *Noah's Ark* in October 2009.

• Judge **Liza N. Burby** (Children's/Young Adult Fiction) is the author of *How to Publish Your Children's Book* (Square One Publishers), 38 nonfiction children's books, and one YA novel. She is also an award-winning freelance journalist. Learn more at lizaburby.com, where you can sign up for an e-newsletter about the children's book industry.

• Judge **Ann Byle** (Inspirational Writing) is author of *The Making of a Christian Bestseller* (FaithWalk) and coauthor with surfer Bethany Hamilton of *Devotions for the Soul Surfer* (Thomas Nelson). Her book *Plainfield Township* (Arcadia) was released in June 2008. She is a freelance reporter and editor, and reviews religious books for *Publishers Weekly*.

• Judge **James Cummins** (Rhyming Poetry) is the author of five books of poems, most recently *Then and Now* (Swallow Press/Ohio University Press, 2004) and *Jim and Dave Defeat the Masked Man*, co-authored with David Lehman (Soft Skull Press, 2005). He has an MFA from the University of Iowa's Writers' Workshop and is the curator of the Elliston Poetry Collection at the University of Cincinnati, where he is also a professor of English. His first book, *The Whole Truth* (North Point Press, 1986), was a sequence of sestinas, a type of Troubadour, formal poem. He lives in Cincinnati with his wife, Maureen Bloomfield, a poet and art critic, and their two daughters.

• Judge **Miriam Sagan**'s (Non-Rhyming Poetry) newest book of poetry is *Map of the Lost* (University of New Mexico Press, 2008). She founded and runs the creative writing program at Santa Fe Community College. She has recently been a writer in residence at Everglades National Park, Petrified Forest National Park and THE LAND/an art site, where she has been working on poetry about ecological issues and land use.

• Judge **Julie Wheeler** (Feature Article) is a creative writing and composition instructor for the University of Colorado. She has authored countless columns and feature articles on a wide range of high-tech topics, and she is a co-author of *The Keys to Success Reader* (Prentice Hall, 1998).

• Judge **Aury Wallington** (Stage Play) is the author of the *New York Times* Bestseller *Saving Charlie* (Del Ray, 2007). Her TV credits include *Sex and the City* and *Veronica Mars*. Her one-woman show, *Virgin of the Vieux Carre*, had a sold-out run at the People's Playhouse in New York in 2003. She currently has two TV pilots in development at ABC Family and the USA network.

• Judge **Chad Gervich** (Television/Movie Script) is a television producer, published author, and award-winning playwright. He created and produced the Style Network's hit comedy/reality series, *Foody Call*, and executive-produced *Celebrity Drive-By*, a talk show pilot for E! Entertainment. He has also developed and produced Internet series for Fox and Warner Brothers, and he's currently writing for *Reality Binge*, a talk/sketch show on Fox Reality Channel. You can read more from Chad on *Script Notes*, *Writers Digest's* screenwriting blog at blog.writersdigest.com/scriptnotes, or in Chad's book, *Small Screen, Big Picture: A Writers Guide to the TV Business* (Three Rivers, 2008).

Finally, our most heartfelt congratulations to the winners and the more than 17,000 entrants in this year's competition. The quality of your entries makes the judging more difficult each year. We look forward to seeing your work in the 78th Annual *Writer's Digest* Writing Competition Collection.

TABLE OF CONTENTS

THE MISTRESS OF WHOLESOME

Jacob M. Appel
New York, NY

THE CAST:
MARGARET, a cardiologist's wife (F-late 30s)
GWEN, a cardiologist's mistress (F-30s)
CONNIE CALLARD, an adoption agent (F-20s)

THE SETTING:
The entire play takes place on the lower story of Margaret and Leland's upscale, Washington, D.C., condominium: a living room with attached kitchenette. Sliding glass doors run along the back wall of the condo, opening onto a spacious patio; while most of the patio cannot be seen, one might consider placing a few potted plants behind the glass to remind the audience of what lies beyond. A front door opens at stage right. The living room is furnished in the modernist style (sofa, coffee table, Barcelona chairs, end table with lamp and telephone), but the space appears cold and austere, with few personal effects. It should mirror the state of Margaret and Leland's marriage. In one corner of the living room, a framed painting conceals a wall safe; alternatively, a freestanding safe is visible. The kitchenette appears immaculately clean and well ordered, as pristine as a model kitchen in a showroom. As the play progresses, the condo slowly descends into chaos.

CURTAIN RISES:
It is mid-afternoon. Gwen appears outside the sliding doors in a trench coat, carrying an oversized handbag, appearing both sexually alluring and world-weary—the sort of woman who has been around the block so many times, she has worn down the pavement. Gwen knocks on the glass. She waits, but nobody answers. She peers into the condo, holding her hand above her eyes like a visor. Then she tries the lock. Finally, she picks up a nearby shovel and bashes a hole in the glass, reaches inside and unlocks the door. She turns on the table lamps and admires the condo. Next, she enters the kitchen and rummages through the drawers until she finds scissors. She leaves the drawers open and uses the scissors to sever the telephone lines in both the kitchen and living room. She looks at her watch, visibly impatient. Finally, she rifles through the refrigerator/freezer and removes a pint-sized container of ice cream. When she opens the lid to serve herself, jewelry pours out of the container. No ice cream! She returns to the refrigerator/freezer several times and removes

4

additional food packages (a box of popsicles, a carton of cereal), but each contains only more jewelry. Gwen is glaring at the jewelry with mounting hunger and frustration when Margaret enters the condo through the front door. Margaret is the quintessential suburban matron, deeply concerned with appearances; her body clings desperately to its last vestiges of youth, while her soul is already well entrenched in middle age. All that Margaret's tableau lacks is a child following at her heels. Or possibly five. At first, Margaret does not notice Gwen. She removes her jacket and hangs it on a hook. When she does see Gwen, she tries to mask her concern.

MARGARET

May I help you with something?

GWEN

You're out of ice cream.

MARGARET

Let me try that again: Who are you and what are you doing in my kitchen?

GWEN

Is that any way to treat a guest? Honestly, the least
you could do is offer me a snack...

MARGARET

Do I know you?

GWEN

That's beside the point, isn't it? You have a houseguest on the brink of keeling over from starvation. Most people would find me something to eat.

MARGARET

You're *not* my guest. You have to be *invited* to be a guest. If you were a guest—

GWEN

—I'd settle for a blueberry muffin and a cup of tea—

MARGARET

If you were a guest—someone I had *invited* into my home—I would certainly offer you a snack... a cup of tea, or even a cocktail, and an assortment of Italian pastries, and I'd ask after our mutual friends and acquaintances. But we don't have any mutual friends and acquaintances, because you're not my guest, because *I don't know you*... Do I?

GWEN

If you were *my* guest, I'd certainly offer *you* something.

MARGARET

My husband didn't bring you back here, did he?
(Shouting)
Leland! Goddamit, Leland! Get your philandering ass out here and explain yourself.

GWEN

I'm all alone... And for the record, if you *were* my guest, I wouldn't start accusing you of things before I'd even offered you a cup of tea and a blueberry muffin.

MARGARET

I'll bear that in mind. Now kindly explain what you're doing here.

GWEN

You should be thankful I'm not a burglar. Who still hides jewelry in the freezer? This is the twenty-first century. If I were a thief, that's the first place I'd look.

MARGARET

(Obviously lying)
Who would want these old things anyway? They're paste—every last one. Not worth a pint of ice cream.

GWEN

Then why hide them in the freezer?

MARGARET

Why hide them in the freezer...? I'm afraid that's none of your business... Now you have exactly ten seconds to account for your presence in my house or I'm going to telephone the police. Am I making myself clear?

GWEN

You wouldn't believe how famished I am. I always get hungry when I'm nervous. Do you really have Italian pastries?
(Gwen returns to the refrigerator and empties the contents aphazardly onto the countertop. She finds additional valuables—maybe gold watches, silver candlesticks, even stacks of currency—but still no food.)

MARGARET

(Her frustration increasing.)
For Christ's sake, this is not a soup kitchen. Could you please stop making a mess of my things? I'm expecting company.
(Margaret begins repacking the jewelry into the food cartons as Gwen continues to empty the cabinets.)
We had the cleaning lady in this morning... And now everything's ruined! Ruined!
(Margaret gives up repacking the jewelry, unable to keep up with

Gwen's plundering.)
Goddammit! Would you mind telling me *how* you got in here?

GWEN
I picked the lock…
(Margaret notices the shattered glass. Now she is more visibly alarmed.)

MARGARET
So you are a burglar!

GWEN
Please calm down. I'm sorry about the door…

MARGARET
Do you know how much those panes cost? That's Italian glass!

GWEN
(Gwen topples pots and pans from the shelves.)
You don't even have any crackers or canned fruit. What would you do in an emergency? If you were trapped here during an influenza pandemic or a nuclear attack. How would you eat?

MARGARET
This really is too much. My husband will be home soon…

GWEN
I thought you were going to phone the police.

MARGARET
He's a large man—a large, muscular man who always carries a concealed handgun…

GWEN
There's no point in lying to me, Margaret. You're a terrible liar.

MARGARET
You're forcing my hand…Ten…Nine…Eight…
(Gwen joins in the counting)

MARGARET & GWEN
Seven…Six…Five…
(Margaret stops counting and glares at Gwen.)

MARGARET
(Angrily, after a pause)
… One…Zero.
(Margaret reaches for the telephone; she attempts desperately to

secure a dial tone.)
Operator? Operator?

GWEN
Don't bother. I already cut the lines.

MARGARET
You what?!

GWEN
It's not a big deal. They do it all the time in movies.

MARGARET
Very well. There's a donut shop on the corner...I'm
going to go get the police...
    (Margaret retrieves her jacket.)

GWEN
I thought you were expecting company.
    (Margaret realizes that if she leaves the apartment, she may miss her
    visitor. She returns the jacket to the hook.)

MARGARET
What do you want from me?

GWEN
From you? Nothing. But I do have bad news for you, Margaret...

MARGARET
What sort of bad news? And how do you know my name?

GWEN
Very bad news. Do you really want to know the truth?

MARGARET
If it means that you'll leave before my visitor shows up.

GWEN
Brace yourself for this... I'm your sister.

MARGARET
Fiddlesticks.

GWEN
No, really. I was born the year after you, but our mother couldn't handle two
babies, so she put me up for adoption...

MARGARET

That is complete and total bullshit.

GWEN

Listen to me, Margaret Claypool... Whether you like it or not, I'm your long-lost baby sister and I tracked you down because I was recently diagnosed with a rare, often fatal genetic illness, and the odds are that you're suffering from it too... I felt a duty—a familial obligation—to warn you.

MARGARET

I need to sit down.
     (Margaret sits down.)
I'm feeling a bit dizzy.

GWEN

Can I offer you a cocktail or an Italian pastry?

MARGARET

You're really *my sister*?

GWEN

No. That *was* complete bullshit. I just made that up to frighten you.

MARGARET

     (Suddenly enraged.)
Enough already! I don't know who you are or what you want, but my husband will be here at any moment, and he's a "shoot now and ask questions later" kind of guy.

GWEN

Leland? Leland couldn't shoot a wild boar if it attacked him in his own bed. He's far too indecisive...

MARGARET

Since when are *you* an authority on *my* husband?

GWEN

I'm his mistress.

MARGARET

     (Shocked, but determined to save face.)
Nonsense!... My husband is as faithful as a sheepdog.

GWEN

A moment ago he was a philandering ass.

MARGARET

That was just a figure of speech…

GWEN

I've been sleeping with your husband for eleven years, Margaret. That's a lot more than a figure of speech.

MARGARET

Goodness… .Leland's mistress…

GWEN

Gwen Ermont… It's so good to finally meet you after all this time.
        (Gwen extends her hand, but Margaret ignores it.)
I've heard *so* much about you… All good… Or *almost* all good. If it were *all* good, I suppose Leland wouldn't be sleeping with me… Anyway, if you don't mind my saying so, you're extremely fortunate to be married to a man who thinks so highly of you.

MARGARET

        (Slowly recovering)
Leland's mistress? Why didn't you say so?… But you're so…

GWEN

You expected someone younger?

MARGARET

Yes… And prettier.

GWEN

That's not a pleasant thing to say to the woman you're sharing a husband with.

MARGARET

You really do have to leave. Immediately.

GWEN

I will. As soon as we've had a brief heart-to-heart chat.
        (Gwen continues to remove food packages from shelves, periodically
        discovering more valuables. Still no food.)
Don't you have anything at all to eat in this house?

MARGARET

We order a lot of take-out…Leland often won't come home until very late.

GWEN

Because he's detained at the hospital…?

MARGARET

(Refusing Gwen's bait)

That's the life of a cardiologist. Even with the sun down, hearts still need mending... What kind of wife would I be if I begrudged him his time at the hospital?

(Margaret returns some jewelry to the freezer.)

Can you please stop making a wreck of things?

GWEN

Don't you have any leftovers stashed away somewhere? Or gourmet items? Gift-wrapped chocolates? Easter confections?

MARGARET

No. We don't. And you really must go. Come back tomorrow and I'll prepare you a steak dinner or ham-and-eggs or whatever you want—you can bash open the eiderdown pillows and pour condiments onto the bed linens for all I care—and we can talk until your tongue swells up so large that you asphyxiate on it—but right now you'll have to leave. I have an extremely important appointment this afternoon. A *private* appointment.

GWEN

Aren't you even the slightest bit curious about my relationship with Leland? Don't you want to know how we met—or what he sees in me that he doesn't see in you?

MARGARET

Write me a note... Do you have stationery?

(Margaret stuffs a stack of stationery into Gwen's hands)

Here you go. My own monogrammed writing paper. From Veronica's on M Street. Why don't you write me a tell-all letter and bring it back tomorrow...? Or better yet, mail it... I'll get you a stamp.

(Margaret searches her purse for a stamp, but finds none. Eventually, she deposits several coins on the kitchen table.)

Here's forty-one cents. That's the best I can do.

GWEN

(Gwen continues to ransack the cabinets for food while she speaks.)

It started the summer after I finished my acting degree at Vassar. We were sitting next to each other on a plane, flying back from Bridgeport, Connecticut. Leland had been rendezvousing with a pharmaceuticals salesgirl he'd met at a diabetes convention—I think you were at your aunt's funeral that weekend, if I remember it correctly—and I was returning from putting the finishing touches on the National Dwarf Hall of Fame... That's what I do for a living. I'm a curator-for-hire. A museum mercenary.

MARGARET

Please listen to me. This is no ordinary visitor. I really must make a good impression.

GWEN

Tom Thumb was born in Bridgeport. You know, the tiny guy from the P. T. Barnum circus. As far as I'm concerned, it's as fitting a place for a Dwarf Hall of Fame as any, although—if you want get all technical about it—Thumb wasn't actually a dwarf. He was a midget.

MARGARET

This could be the most important appointment of my adult life. What can I do to convince you to leave?

GWEN

Small difference, if you ask me. But these little people get all worked up about these things… My point is that I started talking to your husband, and I fell for him so quickly that when he told me he was a cardiologist, I pretended to have a heart attack. Right there in the main cabin. And it worked, too. It's the only time in my life that my acting degree ever paid off… After we'd made an emergency landing in Philadelphia, Leland rode with me to the hospital in the ambulance… It was only later—once we'd fallen in love—that he admitted he knew I was faking. That's what I admire about Leland: He's the sort of man who lets you fake a heart attack for him.

MARGARET

I'm glad you and my husband are so happy together.

GWEN

But we're not happy. Not any more…

MARGARET

Then I'm sorry you and my husband aren't happy together.

GWEN

(Growing desperate.)
You have to help me. Please. I'm begging you.

MARGARET

How can I possibly help *you*?

GWEN

May I speak to you candidly: mistress to wife?

MARGARET

(Margaret sweeps up the broken window glass.)
I'm going to put all of my cards on the table: Leland and I are trying to adopt a baby. A social worker from the adoption agency will be arriving here in less than ten minutes to see if our home is fit for a child—to evaluate our parental suitability. She doesn't want to hear about how *you* met my husband.

GWEN

I think Leland is falling out of love with me. I'm afraid he's already fallen in love with another woman...

MARGARET

Look, I'm sure you're just imagining things. My husband doesn't have a cheating bone in his body—or at least not *that* many of them. But in any case, all of this is between you and Leland. I want absolutely nothing to do with it. I don't want to hear about it. I don't want to know about it.

GWEN

Please, Margaret. I'm not sure where else to turn... and even though this is the first time I've ever met you face to face, I guess I feel like we're old friends... I remember how I sat up beside the telephone past midnight when you had your gallbladder surgery, waiting for Leland to let me know that you were okay... and that time you sliced your finger open on the rusty faucet and you thought you'd contracted tetanus...

MARGARET

You know about all that?

GWEN

Leland tells me everything.

MARGARET

Well, Leland tells me nothing. Which is how I prefer it... And you and I are not old friends. This is *not* a social relationship... Wives do not have social relationships with their husband's mistresses—at least not if they're aware of it.
    (A long pause.)

GWEN

Doesn't it bother you?

MARGARET

    (Feigning ignorance)
Doesn't *what* bother me?

GWEN

That your husband thinks about *me* when he's having sex with *you*.

MARGARET

I thought he was thinking about a third woman when he has sex with both of us.

GWEN

How can you be so detached?

13

MARGARET

How can I *not* be? You don't think I realized a long time ago that Leland has been less than faithful? The wife always knows—even if she chooses not to admit it... Women who claim they're shocked when they discover that their husbands have other wives and children in different states are lying through their teeth... or they've tricked themselves into not knowing what they actually do know... Deep down they *always* know. They're just reluctant to tamper with the status quo, because they're afraid things might get worse... That they might end up with nothing at all... In any case, I gave up on controlling my husband's more unpleasant urges a long time ago... What I want now is a beautiful bouncing baby girl from China who looks absolutely nothing like her father. *Leland owes me that.*

GWEN

There is no third woman. That's the worst part.

MARGARET

But you just said—

GWEN

It's *you*, Margaret. I think Leland has fallen back in love with you.

MARGARET

My husband? In love with *me*?

GWEN

It's hard to believe, isn't it? But when you started planning to adopt the baby, you put a lot of crazy ideas into his head. About reforming himself. About becoming a model parent and all that bullshit.

MARGARET

Did Leland really tell you that?

GWEN

You don't know what I've been going through, Margaret. Leland and I have been together for *eleven* years. That's a third of my life. And now he expects me to stand idly by while he throws everything away for some stranger's baby?

MARGARET

Wait a second—

GWEN

No, you wait a second! I've played fair by you all these years. I never asked Leland to leave you—I'm not that kind of woman. I respected what was yours, and I trusted that you'd respect what was mine. The way I thought about it was that we each had our own niche. Like different species of birds who share different portions of the same habitat. Leland wanted one woman who was sensuous and magnetic and exhilarating in bed... and another who kept her pearls in the freezer and used expressions like "fiddlesticks"... It all felt very mature, very civilized, almost French... You should be ashamed to leave me out in the cold like this! After all I've done for you! After all we've been through together!

MARGARET

I'm not doing anything to you. Is it my fault if Leland's had a change of heart?

GWEN

It's unfair, I tell you. Why should love be first-come, first-served? Like waiting in line for a sandwich at the deli. What right do you have? Do you really think you own him just because you started sleeping with him before I did? I love him *more* than you do. That's what should matter.

MARGARET

So what do you expect me to do? Leland's a grown adult. He's capable of making his own decisions. Honestly, I don't understand why you've come here.

GWEN

I'll tell you why. Because I want Leland to love me again... I *need* Leland to love me again. And you're going to find a way to make that happen.

MARGARET

How am I supposed to do that? I can't even get Leland to tuck in the shower curtain.

GWEN

You'll find a way. He *is* your husband.
	(Gwen removes a musket from her handbag.)
And if you don't—Well, let's just say you will...

MARGARET

You're not really threatening to shoot me with *that*?

GWEN

You bet I am. But only if I have to... It allegedly belonged to Paul Revere. I borrowed it from Special Exhibits at the Smithsonian.
	(She loads the musket with grapeshot and powder.)
As guns go, it may be not glamorous—but rest assured, it's one hundred percent functional. A woman like me doesn't have much access to sophisticated weaponry on a daily basis. She's got to take her arms where she finds them.

MARGARET

Let me get this straight: If I can't convince my husband to fall back in love with you, you're going to shoot me with a Revolutionary War musket.

GWEN
Right between the eyes. And then I'm going to shoot myself... If I can't have Leland, nobody will.

MARGARET
Look, Gwen. I honestly wish I could help you. But you know how stubborn Leland can be... Once he's made up his mind, there's nothing to be done about it.

GWEN
Well, you'd better figure something out. I'm telling you, I'm desperate.

MARGARET
Leland's going to be here any minute. I'll talk to him... We can all sit down together sometime soon and hash this out...

GWEN
Leland's not coming.

MARGARET
Oh, he'll be here. He wants this baby as much as I do...

GWEN
He can't come.

MARGARET
What do you mean: 'He *can't* come'?

GWEN
He has a competing obligation.

MARGARET
What sort of 'competing obligation'?

GWEN
He's in the trunk of my car...

MARGARET
You're joking again.

GWEN
He stopped by the International Barbecue Museum this morning... that's where I'm setting up the vintage grill exhibit... and I was afraid he might break things off with me, so when he turned around, I swatted him over the head with President Johnson's personal spatula and wrapped him up in Katherine

Hepburn's garden hose.

MARGARET

Leland is really in the trunk of your car??

GWEN

Don't worry. It's a large trunk. He's got enough air to last him several hours.

MARGARET

(Looking at her watch)

So he's going to miss our appointment. That bastard!

[EXERPT FROM STAGE PLAY]

A PERFECTION OF WISDOM

Tom Clark
Loveland, OH

There was an unnatural twist in the narrow aluminum ladder. Lhakpa felt his weight suddenly shift over the deep crevice. Cautiously, he eased forward. The ladder's edge bit again into the melting snow.

It was the team's second day on the Khumbu Glacier, a frozen river of ice near the foot of Mount Everest. Base Camp was still 17,000 feet above. No one knew exactly how deep the crevices were—some Sherpas believe that those who fall will end up in the Americas.

Lhakpa's uncle leaned backward and buried his crampons beneath the snow. He tightened his grip on the safety line.

"Come on, Lhakpa. Let's go! I have you!" he said.

Back home Lhakpa's mother made arrangements with the Buddhist monks to say prayers for Lhakpa's safe return. They would spin Mani wheels and light butter lamps in honor of Chenrezig, the enlightened being of Compassion. It was Chenrezig who would deliver them from suffering. She understood the dangers, but it did not make her worry any less.

Lhakpa stood motionless on the ladder. His heart was pounding in his chest.

"What's wrong?" his uncle called out.

"I can't do it," Lhakpa yelled back.

His uncle paused. "Use the safety lines," he said.

Gritting his teeth, Lhakpa slowly moved his right foot forward. He could feel the ladder wobble again.

"Keep going!" his uncle yelled.

On his last step Lhakpa felt something different. It was the snow beneath his feet. He had made it.

Night was approaching. Lhakpa and his uncle set up their tent near the foot of the Everest. The howling wind was merciless. It clawed and gashed its way across their skin.

"We might as well be on the moon," his uncle said. Off in the distance swirls of snow were being kicked off of the mountain's ridge. It was a sobering reminder of the dangers to come.

Once inside they started boiling some water for tea. "So, how's your mother?" Lhakpa's uncle asked.

"She's fine," Lhakpa replied. "She prays twice a day. Three times since I joined the team."

His uncle smiled. "She's only being protective of you," he said.

Lhakpa sighed. "I know, but since father died that's all she does."

His uncle nodded his head.

Lhakpa became silent for a moment. "What was he like?"

His uncle paused. "Your father?" he said.

He checked the water in the pot.

Lhakpa nodded as his uncle motioned for Lhakpa to pass him a cup.

"He was a good climber, but an even greater man. Something you rarely see nowadays," he said.

He took a sip of his tea. "I remember when the great climber Pemba Dorie was building his team for his record climb. Your father was the first one he selected."

After supper, as Lhakpa and his uncle turned in, the light from the full moon gave the snow a blue tint. As he lay in his sleeping bag, Lhakpa's mind flashed back to 10 years ago at his parents' house. It was late. He and his younger brother, Phurba, had just gone to bed. They were awakened by a knock on the front door. As they peered out through their bedroom door they could see their two uncles. Their faces were sad.

"What are they saying?" Phurba whispered.

"Shh! Just watch," Lhakpa snapped.

Their mother became very quiet. She turned away and sat down on a nearby chair.

"Do you think something happened to father?" asked his brother.

"No. I don't know. Maybe," Lhakpa said.

A tragic accident had occurred at the Khumbu Glacier. A large tower of ice had toppled onto another creating a domino effect, burying a team of Nepali Sherpas. His father was missing.

"Helpless," his uncle described. "There was no time to run."

Then something interrupted Lhakpa's thoughts. It sounded like a faint voice coming from outside the tent. "Who would be outside at this time?" he thought.

His uncle lay fast asleep. Lhakpa pulled on his jacket, slipped on his boots and stepped outside. He heard it again, turned around and looked up. It was coming from the Lhotse Face, a 4,000-foot vertical rock wall on the north side of Everest.

He couldn't believe it. A team of climbers was attempting a dangerous late-night ascent in high winds. They were just below the yellow, limestone band midway around the mountain. One of the team members with his hand on a tethered line was waving an ice axe over his head. He couldn't make out what he was saying, but it seemed directed toward Lhakpa.

Just then Lhakpa felt a hand on his shoulder. It was his uncle. "What's wrong?" he asked.

"There are climbers on the mountain," Lhakpa said pointing upwards.

His uncle strained to see. "What climbers?"

They were gone.

Lhakpa blinked his eyes. "They were there a minute ago."

The next morning the team awoke well before sunrise. At one of the nearby ice columns, several members refitted their crampons and used ice axes to work their way up the vertical face. Fascinated, Lhakpa watched as small shrouds of ice rained down on him.

"You might want to step away a bit," his uncle warned.

"I'm ok," said Lhakpa. "I think I'll just stay and watch."

By mid-morning the sun's rays were slowly emerging from the top of the column. It felt good on Lhakpa's face. Suddenly, there was a loud crack that made his heart jump. He looked up at the two climbers. One of them seemed to be losing his balance and falling backward. The other climber was holding on to both axes, bracing himself. In a split second the wall of ice exploded around him and came crashing downward.

Back home his mother was preparing a meal. She felt anxious. As she reached for a clay pot, the cupboard suddenly collapsed. Phurba came rushing in. She was standing over a large pile of broken clay and glass. He could see the anguish in her eyes.

"Lhakpa!" she whispered.

All was quiet. There was no blue sky. No climbers. Only the dark milky white snow surrounded him. Lhakpa turned his head and saw his gloved hand. As he pushed away some of the snow, he discovered several large blocks of ice had formed a pocket over him. It was tight, but he managed to clear enough snow to free his other arm.

Outside, rescuers radioed nearby teams for assistance. "Lhakpa!" his uncle yelled. "Lhakpa!"

He frantically searched every opening he could find. "Helpless," he would later describe it. "It happened so quick."

Lhakpa's feet were pinned against one of the ice blocks. He tried to jerk them free. Nothing budged. He leaned backwards and closed his eyes to think. When he opened them, something metallic caught his eye. He reached over and gave it a pull. An ice axe?

Details were sketchy from incoming transmissions back home... Large ice collapse at Khumbu glacier... Half a dozen injured... Several missing... Lhakpa's mother's heart sank. Down at the base camp the Himalayan Rescue Association started making preparations to clear a flat area for use as a helicopter pad.

Back at the glacier, several team members were located and stabilized. Lhakpa, however, was still missing. With each passing minute his chance for survival dropped.

His uncle continued to scan the area. About halfway up he noticed something moving above the pile of ice and snow. It looked like a gloved hand. He yelled to some of the other rescuers to follow him.

"Lhakpa! Lhakpa!" he called out.

Several hours later, back at the rescue station, rescuers loaded the last of the injured onto the helicopter. Lhakpa watched from the window of the clinic with his uncle. As far as the doctors could tell, aside from a few deep bruises, nothing was broken. "That could have been me," he said quietly.

"Maybe it wasn't your time," his uncle replied. He looked down and noticed Lhakpa was holding an ice axe. It looked different. "Souvenir?" he asked.

Lhakpa handed it to him. "I used this to dig myself out."

He held it up. It looked different than the one they had brought.

"This is an older model," said his uncle. "See the metal head? It's called a banana blade. Normally it's used to climb step inclines where the surface of the snow is very hard and brittle."

Lhakpa remembered what he had seen on the Lhotse Face a few days earlier. He told his uncle one of the climbers was waving similar ice axe over his head. The odd thing was they were climbing so late at night. It reminded his uncle of a story he heard long ago.

"A non-climber asked a group of Sherpas one day, 'Why do you climb?' No one could answer, except one, an elder Sherpa. He said a climber needs six perfections to reach fulfillment at the summit: giving, morality, patience, vigor, contemplation and wisdom. The most important of these is wisdom. It lets you see things as they really are. Even as the body withers on Chomolungma (Everest) the soul must continue to climb."

His uncle flipped the axe over and something caught his eye. There were five deliberate etchings across the handle about a centimeter apart.

"What's wrong?" asked Lhakpa.

His uncle hesitated. "See this?" he said pointing to the handle. "The last time I saw markings like this was the day your father disappeared. He made them to identify his equipment from others on the team. He said the marks represented five of the six perfections of wisdom."

His uncle handed the axe back to Lhakpa. "Maybe your father is among the mountain gods now."

MY CUP RUNNETH UNDER

April Love Bailey
Miramar, FL

Female breasts seem to be getting more than their fair share of attention these days, from women as much as men. The "bigger is better" mentality in the United States has led to a glut of breast implant surgeries, once known as the "boob job" but now tempered with more gentle terminology such as breast "enhancement," "enlargement," or "augmentation." Within the last few years, this surgery has become the leading cosmetic procedure according to the American Society of Plastic Surgeons, with 329,000 women receiving implants in 2006, up more than 55 percent from 2000, and expected to continue rising.

Whether natural or surgically altered, buxom women are filling and spilling out of their C cups, D cups and beyond, epitomizing super-sexuality in films, television, music videos, and prints ads everywhere on earth. It seems, more often than not, that large-breasted women are considered the sexual ideal, their heaving bosoms the magic accessories selling everything from sports equipment to clothing to family vacations. So, what about the small-chested rest of us? With the bosom-obsessed masses celebrating, marketing, and proudly exhibiting ample breasts, it raises an obvious yet often unvoiced question. Are some women actually content with, and thankful for, their modest, undoctored cleavage? Let me be one—of many, I am certain—to stand up and say *absolutely*!

Growing up the only girl in a family of boys, I never gave breasts a thought, not one moment's contemplation. I was that goofy kid who poked bras at department stores, giggling about the row of concave cups left in my wake. Such garments had no connection with me, and served as mere toys for my amusement until my own bosom ceased to be flat. I had previously been quite content with the uncomplicated state of my chest, and with three older brothers, I fit in well, more like a fourth brother than the baby sister. That all changed the day our teenaged neighbor, Netra, noticed—and announced quite publicly—my sprouting anthills.

Shockingly shapely and about four years my senior, Netra lived across the street from my family. By the age of 13 or 14, she already had woman-sized curves and an impressive rack. Well, it seemed impressive to my nine-year-old eyes, especially when she hefted the pair up with her forearms one day and let them plop on a table at the library. I had never witnessed such blatant interaction with one's private anatomy before. Even back then, in the mid-1970s, Netra seemed breast-obsessed, repositioning hers like luggage and feeling the need to proclaim my budding womanhood to every kid in the neighborhood. I was nine and those freaking anthills stuck out like singing warts beneath my shirt. Why, oh, why did they have to do that, and wasn't there some kind of cream to make them go away?

But on they grew, slowly, steadily, as did the rest of my body into my tenth and eleventh years. I wore the contraption known as the training bra, resenting it less and less as it filled. My flat-chested girlfriends marveled at my early buds, so, for a few years, until about the age of 12, I resigned myself to being the big-boobed girl in the group.

I remember distinctly the moment my busty self-image was challenged and reset in the opposite direction. High school, junior year, 1982. Strolling through the mall with a guy friend, I spotted an adorable strapless dress in a store window, and commented on its beauty.

"Yeah," he said, snickering, "but what would you hold it up with?"

I paused but did not respond, thinking to myself, *Oh, he cannot be talking about me! I'm the big-boobed girl.*

This jeer may have been the first pebble in the avalanche of my physical reeducation, but it took years for me to fully accept that my chest was no longer huge. In fact, it was not even considered large anymore. Somewhere between 12 and 16, my body had caught up to—and some might argue, surpassed—my breasts.

There were other remarks throughout my adolescence about my lack of "action" up top, but no amount of flat-chested razzing could ever erase the feeling I had as a freakishly buxom nine-year-old. During those few formative years, I hated being the big-boobed girl, and discovering in adulthood that I barely fit a B cup felt to me like winning the lottery. I shopped for undergarments in the little girls department because the women's bras, with those reinforced hooks, thick padding, and all that lace, felt overly bulky for the job I needed them to do. Snatching up a bulk pack of sports bras, which worked great for non-sports-related activities too, proved much simpler. It took me eight seconds to stock up on three years' worth of bras, and I could have sworn the Hallelujah Chorus rang out from the store's sound system.

By the time I reached my thirties, I decided to spice things up by investing in some "grown-up lady bras," and headed to the Mecca of unmentionables: Victoria's Secret. Two bras and sixty bucks later (a far cry from a sporty three-pack for $9.99), I found myself outfitted comfortably with a brassiere that described its padding as "nipple coverage." Felt like plain old padding to me. So much so, that now when I wear my VS special, I still ask my husband, "Do I look huge in this?" He just laughs and leaves the room. Other attempts at purchasing sexy, adult bras left me with scratches from fancy stitching and gapping in the cup. Gapping?! Are bra manufacturers making B cups roomier these days?

My husband, Jerry, sometimes teases me, insisting that my "killer Bs" would be more aptly named "The A Team," but I could hardly imagine gazing down upon anything larger than a handful—my hand, not Jerry's. All right, I joke about being small, but to this day I celebrate my diminutive "girls." I don't need them flopping about, broadcasting my gender through clingy sweaters and bustiers. To me, sexy is more a state of mind than a state of body and, while my cup may not runneth over, I feel feminine and as alluring as I care to feel. Besides, I have never suffered from breast-induced backaches, bra straps digging trenches into my shoulders, or men aiming conversations at my chest instead of my face (well, once, but the guy was wickedly flirtatious and enticed by my low-cut blouse).

Teenage girls and young women worry enough about their appearance. So, to my low-cup sisters, if family, friends or the advertising world has never told you, it is okay to be small. You're okay. This may seem simple, but it's a powerful realization. While my figure might never reach bombshell proportions, my breasts are the ideal size for me. They never get in the way, allowing me to sleep face down, emulate Prince convincingly at masquerade parties, and wear halter-tops without fear of a wardrobe malfunction. They don't beat me when I run, and virtually disappear when I lie down. Love that!

Although I am content with my bust, I could not fault anyone for getting implants. If a woman feels unattractive with a small chest, and more attractive with larger breasts, then more power to her. In the grand scheme of things, the size of my boobs is really not that big a deal to me. My experience in childhood probably helped shaped my view, but I feel as much a woman with my bosom locked and loaded as if I wore the pair like an Oscar-night accessory. Thanks to the early onset of puberty and perhaps Netra's big mouth, I had my fill of buxom babe status as a pre-teen. Even now, wearing one of my padded bras, I feel conspicuous, as if my weirdly perched cones call forth for the entire world to behold. Perhaps one of my VS specials will make its way around my ribcage for a special occasion, or under a loose-fitting dress. In everyday life? No, thanks. Just bring on one of my comfy sports bras, for I am no longer the big-boobed girl. Talk about getting something off my chest!

EVERY SHINY THING

R.K. Chandler
Monterey, CA

A skinny man in green polyester, Goodwill clothes, visible stitching in the lapels, jail-time face: pores, a scar. Not middle aged but getting there. A reek coming off him in the dead-of-January air, and it isn't Goodwill but a creepiness, a preternatural silence like that of a stalking animal, only he isn't stalking, he isn't in the shadows, he's in broad daylight, in the mid-morning gloom, in bright green like some sort of leprechaun on her porch, holding a Bible, and he's the first person she's seen in a week, and maybe that's why she says Come in.

He stands there a moment, as though she might have been addressing someone else. Turns sideways, as though Someone Else were there beside him, and she sees it: the stomach. Not just a gut, but something serious, a tumor, no, much larger: he's pregnant looking, the stomach so distended it puts her in mind of those children in third-world countries, so undernourished their stomach muscles can't hold their guts in place and they sag.

You heard me, she says. Come in.

He nods, and she moves aside so he can enter her tiny house. He steps over the threshold and floorboards groan under carpet fibers.

Guess you don't get that much, huh, she says. Come in, I mean.

They are nearly face-to-face. His is craggy, rocky, like a telescope picture of the moon's surface, the whites of his eyes shading to brown from (she knows) the gunk in his system. She holds her breath. Wonders if he can smell her too. Days since she showered, she knows alcohol exudes from her pores, she wonders if her face will end up like his in another decade or two, wonders in a lightning-flash way if even a man like this would want her, not a good thought to have this close up and she hopes it does not transmit from her eyes to his.

Anyway, you can sit down, she says.

He moves slowly, one hand holding the Bible and the other holding the stomach, as though the guts threaten to spill out of his green polyester slacks. His pale green shirt is untucked and she's pretty sure the pants underneath are only half zipped, imagines a gaudy belt buckle straining to hold everything in place. She hears him grunt under his breath as he wobble-walks toward the chair and she says No, the couch, and he goes to it obediently, positions himself the way a pregnant woman does just before sitting, the way she herself had once upon a time positioned herself, putting the one hand behind you for balance, splaying the legs, carefully lowering, letting go at the last instant to let the cushions catch you.

Sorry it's so dark, she says, closing the door. They cut my electric off.

He says nothing, still that silence. She goes to the chair across from him and sits. Lights a cigarette, shakes out the match, says Okay. Get to it.

He swallows. Looks down at the Bible in his hands.

Go ahead, she says.

Still says nothing.

Hello?

He looks up. Grins, brown teeth. Not just a smoker's teeth, teeth, like the face, going to ruin. Hello, he says.

Okay, so you know *that* word, she says. Then she says, I'm sorry. I'm a smartass sometimes.

He still grins, but now he's not looking at her. He's looking past her, behind her at the bookcase, the wall, something. Maybe at Somebody Else, like on the porch.

So, are you going to save my soul, or just sit there creeping me out?

Soul, he says.

Yeah, soul. Start preaching, preacher. I let you into my house, didn't I? So start preaching. What's the problem?

The smile doesn't go anywhere, but the eyes, the eyes flicker now, from her to the something behind her, definitely he's looking at something behind her. She wants to look too. Maybe he has an accomplice, maybe Somebody Else is real. But she doesn't turn. Fuck it. She won't give him the satisfaction if he's trying to scare her. And part of her, a very dark part of her, says Fuck it even if there *is* somebody back there.

Listen, she says. Either get to preaching or leave.

Preaching?

Yeah. Jesus. You know. Isn't that the Word of God you got there?

He looks at the Bible. Then to her. The Word of God, he says.

She puffs a petulant little smoke cloud, an impatient child. The cloud hangs in the dusky air between them, as though trying to resolve itself into a picture both parties can recognize. Are you just going to repeat everything I say? Because that's getting old. Fast.

She reaches down to the side of her chair and lifts a bottle. It's filled with golden liquid. She takes a swig and wags the bottle at him insolently before setting it back down. I'm lost, she says. See? The drinking? The smoking? Letting strange men into my house? Hello?

Hello, he says.

What the fuck's up with you?

His eyes go to the thing behind her and he grins anew.

Okay, she says, feeling the chill along her arm, her spine, a running wildfire of fear. Forget it. Just get out. You're as screwed up as I am. Let me guess. Just got out of the pen, some jail preacher put a Bible in your hand and gave you some clothes, you have to do this shit, I'll have to sign a piece of paper saying you were here so you can show it to your P.O. later. Right?

He grins.

Too many drugs, right? And that stomach. What the hell? I've seen beer bellies, but damn. Look at it.

His grin fades, and she hates herself all over again as he sets the Bible aside and pats his expectant stomach the same way she once did when there were people in her life, before she messed it all up and got to where she is, with the electricity cut off and the house falling apart and her unwashed hair so greasy it looks wet and she doesn't give a damn about anything.

She waves her hand. I'm sorry. I'm mean sometimes. I'm in a lot of pain. Just go. You can leave the Bible or whatever, if that's what you do. Or take it. I don't care.

But he doesn't get up. He sits there, continues rubbing the stomach, almost tenderly. He blinks and she sees it pains him, the stomach, the blink the same way an animal in pain would blink. It's some kind of condition, maybe he's close to dying, maybe the poor idiot is just doing the best he can. Every breath comes as another subliminal groan. And the smell. It's usurped the tiny room. Dark, menstrual. Coming from the deep parts, the bowel parts of him, maybe his soul, decay.

Look, do you need something? she asks. Do you want something?

I want something, he says. And he stands.

The wildfire spreads to her stomach, her own deep parts, her soul if she still has one.

Well, she says, calmly (the way you try to placate a man when you sense they could turn into an animal before your eyes), I don't have any food. Everything in the fridge has gone to shit. No electric, remember? You'll need to leave.

I want something, he repeats, and his eyes go hard.

Leave now, she says, sternly (the second thing you try with them, try to be forceful, make them think twice before they do anything). Leave now or I'll call the law.

But he maintains his glare.

She freezes, or tries to, the cigarette smolders but she only holds it. She's become a small animal in the presence of a larger one. A larger animal who is wounded, even more wounded than she is, who is dangerous. She doesn't even blink. Wants to believe that if she freezes, doesn't move at all, the larger animal will think it's mistaken, nothing's there.

But it's clear he's guessed it, that the phone's cut off too, that she's poor not only in money and spirit but in friends and family and helpful neighbors, she's screwed up everything she ever had, she knows he knows it, from the way he's turning it all over in his mouth, almost chewing on the knowledge, knows it in that fat stomach of his, in his guts, the way an animal just knows because that's the animal's business, to know, to survive.

She thinks of running, but maybe it's not as bad as she fears, she's known some wasteheads in her time, some ex-cons, most of them were okay deep down, she'll give him two or three steps, maybe three and then she'll kick him in the balls, or that stomach, before she flees, goes banging on some stranger's door, involves the law in any way.

It happens before she can react—he takes three steps and more, passes around her, behind her chair, faster than she imagined a wounded animal could move, and she whips her head around to see where he's going. What he's been staring at.

The necklace. On the bookshelf, where she left it after the last fight before he said Fuck off in the amazing way a man could tell you it was over after four years.

The pregnant man stops short of touching it. He bends slightly to eye it, appraise it.

She repositions herself sideways in the chair, letting her bare feet dangle over an arm. Whatever, she says. Take it. Sell it. Get your high. I don't care.

And it's partly true, she doesn't care. The necklace was never really her. A slender, delicate thing, like a gold-plated fettucine noodle, something a rich woman would wear. She wore it once and felt like a fraud. He'd probably stolen it anyway, the fucker.

I said take it, she repeats to the man. It doesn't mean anything to me anymore.

She watches as his bony fingers finally take it, the forefinger and thumb like crab pincers, delicately lifting one end. Lifts it into the air like a jeweler, and even though the light is dull, the necklace seems to shine, a miraculous shine in a room dark as this, it almost looks like the way they light treasure in a movie as it swings gently over his head, above his open mouth. He gapes at heaven like a baby bird. She watches him tongue the tip of it. Lower it, inch by inch, swallowing as he goes. His breathing loud and hungry, an almost sexual breathing, as he draws it into the depths of him, the darkest part of him, until at last he is mouthing his own pincers.

She's standing. What the hell? she says, moving toward the door. What the *hell*?

His eyes are closed, as though savoring. Can't help it, he says. Can't help it. And I've tried.

It's okay, she says. Just please leave.

I've tried, he repeats, opening his eyes.

He turns toward her.

She gets to the door and opens it. It's okay. Just leave.

He takes his time approaching the door, waddle-walking, the floor boards groaning with each step as he nears. Ever since I was a child. A little boy. It's how God made me.

Please. I have friends coming over.

Jewelry, he says.

Please.

Needles. Coins.

Please go.

Every shiny thing, he says, his face in her face, and he shoves her to the floor and slams the door and locks it.

She should have run, should have run, should have run. It's too late now, the larger animal, the one with the gut, like sharks or bears she's read of, eating whatever there is to eat, you slit them open and find beer cans and chicken beaks and fishing tackle, this animal, he has her in his sights. She feels the beginnings of tears, pinpricks in her eyes, ten minutes ago she wanted to die and now all she wants is to live, but it's too late, she should have run, he blurs in the darkness. Your eyes, he says, I love your eyes how they shine.

CHOICES

Diana K. Williams
Crystal Springs, FL

I pushed open the car door and stepped onto the gravel drive. I closed the door behind me, surveying the expanse. The cemetery was bordered by wheat fields on three sides. To my right the green blades blew in the spring sunset; in front of me clouds pushed in.

Twenty-six steps, I thought, looking toward my destination. *Twenty-six steps from the gravel drive to her tombstone.* I took number one.

My foot fell in the tall grass. *The caretaker has gotten lax.* My gaze was fixed on my feet. I took number two.

It had been nineteen years since that morning when the phone rang. A voice simply said, "Cheryl was killed last night in a hunting accident." Step number three.

I recalled my reaction – no words…only silence. The voice went on, "They were hunting for coyotes after midnight. The shotgun accidentally went off inside the vehicle. That's all I know." Step number four.

My dearest friend was dead at age twenty-nine. Her story only partially written. Her potential never realized. Her legacy fixed. Step number five.

My gaze drifted onto a tombstone glistening in the golden glow of the setting sun. It said, "Ed Lafferty born 1930 died 1999." This was a small farming community. That was Freddy's dad. Without stopping I wondered, *Will anyone ever know that he lived? Did he leave behind any mark upon the earth other than this granite headstone?* Step number six.

My eyes slid closed… opening, they caught another stone on my right — "Ethel Shaffer." *She taught me piano for ten years. Will anyone ever know?* Step number seven.

The sunlight kissed my cheek. The breeze from the gray clouds blew my dark hair across my face. My feet moved forward but my stare hung over my shoulder fixed on Ethel's dates — "1899 to 2001." *She lived more than one hundred years on this earth. Did she live the way she wanted to?* Step number eight.

My white, cotton shirt rippled in the breeze. My jacket blew off my shoulders. My eyes circled around to the left. Tim Nackle "1962 to 1976." *He was in my brother's class; killed in an auto accident. Things like that are not supposed to happen in small communities. So much possibility buried in that grave.* Step number nine.

Daffodils pulled my eyes toward the base of Private Tom Handshoe's marker. It read "Killed in combat — WWII." *He died for my freedom. He had* chosen *to die. Am I making choices that show I lived?* Step number ten.

The clouds moved closer, forcing the sunset into darkness. *Light forever battles with darkness; life with death; creation with destruction; decision with indecision.* Step number eleven.

The wind picked up. My hair was aflutter about my face. I pulled my oilskin coat tighter. My brown boot sunk into the dancing grass. My eyes surveyed the expanse of tombstones that stretched up the hill and into the sky. The names were pulling my thoughts back through the decades. *Choices… choices…choices* beat in my spirit. *They are what define us… They determine how we will be remembered.* Step number twelve.

"Asher Ansley 1921 to 1992." That was Sonya's grandfather. She once told me that he had auditioned for lead guitarist of a well-known blues band. They chose someone else but told him he had talent and encouraged him to continue developing it. Instead he took a job in town at the factory… raised a family… went to church each Sunday… then died. *Sonya's mom became a county judge but what if Asher had enlarged his circle of influence? How many unsung songs are in that grave? How many people could he have inspired?* My family tells a story that my uncle played in Sammy Stewart's jazz band in Chicago. One day, the not-yet-famous Louie Armstrong auditioned for a spot in the band. Sammy sent him away. He said Louie couldn't play his style of music. *What if Louie had given up?* Step number thirteen. Step number fourteen.

I peered up at the black clouds, blinking the wind off my eyes. Exhaling, my gaze descended onto the headstone of Ginny Hamilton 1956 to 2002. She was a few years older than me. She lived hard and she lived fast. Crack. Cocaine. Whiskey. Eventual paralysis did not even shake the grip of feeding instant false pleasures into her body. The wheelchair just seemed to inflame the fury inside her; driving her into poverty and eventually the grave. *What burns inside that grave? What undiscovered passion was locked beneath that fury? If she had brought it to fruition would it have changed the world?* Step number fifteen.

Cheryl and I partied with Ginny and her sister once. Fast cars. Fast life. Thank God we couldn't keep up. Thank God for unconscious choices. Step number sixteen… step number seventeen.

The wind whirled. I hardly noticed. My thoughts were running back through life. I saw opportunities to die, opportunities to live, opportunities to be mediocre, opportunities to seize my dreams. Step number eighteen.

God had opened doors. Some I had walked through, others I had pushed shut — out of fear of failure, fear of success, fear of leaving the familiar. Step number nineteen.

A ray of sun pierced through the growing darkness, landing on Cheryl's headstone. From the distance I read "Our Beloved Daughter." Step number twenty.

I had always dreamed of living passionately and with purpose, but I had never mustered the courage to take the risk. For a moment I would dare to walk out on the edge, reaching toward my dreams. But the discomfort of unfamiliar territory forced me back. Instant gratification would beckon me away from God. Arriving at the end of hope reconnected me. The path of least resistance moved me away from the thing I knew I was born to do. Dissatisfaction drew me back. *Unconscious choices are drifting me through life. Unaware they are stealing my potential. My present is the result of yesterday's choices — conscious or not. How I spend each day is determining my reality…establishing my legacy.* Step number twenty-one. Step number twenty-two.

I surveyed the graves toward the valley on my left. I was becoming aware of how much unleashed potential was locked up inside of me because I had not aligned my choices with my greatest desire. *I have been living an unconcentrated life… my actions have not supported my aspirations. Distractions have gone unquestioned. No wonder I feel scattered all over the place. No wonder I'm not progressing toward my desires.* I stopped and began to slowly spin around. *How many misaligned choices lie buried under this earth? How many good intentions to* someday *write those books, paint those masterpieces, or mend those broken relationships were never realized because* life *unconsciously pulled in another direction?*

I saw Harriett Johnson's stone "1940 to 2005." She had the voice of a professional opera singer and never had a lesson. *Why didn't she follow her gift? Didn't she trust God enough to believe it had a purpose? How many souls would she have pierced? How many nations would she have impacted for the God she loved so dearly?* Step number twenty-three.

My eyes closed tight. My face tilted down toward the earth. *Couldn't she recognize the gift inside her?* I pondered in silence. *I recognize the gift inside of me… but what am I doing with it?* The wind gusted; cherry blossoms swirled in the air. The sun refracted blood pink onto Clara Stephens' stone — "1919 to 1995." My heart melted. Step number twenty-four.

Clara was widowed young, sang off key in church, and I doubt she ever traveled beyond the county line. She was an icon in the community not because she raised three successful children alone but because she had a smile for everyone; always had a word to pick you up when you were down. When the Smiths' barn burnt down she baked pies for them. When my best friend did not make the all-star basketball team Clara cheered her up with a story. When my dog died she picked wildflowers for the grave. Everyone loved Clara because Clara loved everyone. *Clara lived and loved the way she wanted to. She chose to live for someone other than herself. Now she lives on because those she touched live on. We are interdependent.* Step number twenty-five.

Choices. I looked around and saw that I was surrounded by the unchangeable legacy of choices. Some had chosen to walk straight and stayed true to the thing God had put them here to do. Some had gotten off course but righted themselves along the way and finished strong. Others had lived their days as though they did not define who they were—what they believed deep down inside themselves. Step number twenty-six.

I slid my hands into my coat pockets. I turned and squarely faced Cheryl's grave. I crouched down. My eyes were on the dates—"1959 to 1988"—but my thoughts were entrenched in contemplation. *If she had lived, would we have been great friends till the end? Would she have dared to change the world with a sudden impact, or even a gentle hug like Clara?*

There have to be so many unrealized dreams, so many desires buried in this cemetery. Why? I suppose the same reason I put off attempting what looks impossible, though I know it is why I am here. The same thing that tethers me to the familiar when I know the unfamiliar holds the fulfillment of my deepest yearnings. I gazed up at the sky. The darkness continued to try and blot out the light as the dark clouds inside me swirled, attempting to put out God's light.

My cheek rested on my clenched hand. My elbow pushed into my thigh. I stared into the stone, reflecting back to the day the eulogist had challenged each of us to not let Cheryl's life be for nothing. Nineteen years had passed and I still did not know how to do that. Nineteen years of going to work, buying things I eventually got rid of, and fading into "normal." Nineteen years of living above average yet below potential. I had come here to remember an old friend. I was beginning to remember me. *Choices. I am surrounded by the outcome of choices. Some made intentionally, others unaware. The end products are either entombed without hope of another chance or enduring on in the lives they have influenced.*

Choices — I am the only one in this cemetery who still has the opportunity to define how I will be known. I could continue to live insulated in a passionless, meandering life or I could choose to unleash the gift inside me. Two paths lay before me. One I could live safely for myself and one day explain to God why I did not trust Him enough to help me attain my potential. The other required unshakable faith to live my dream and impact someone else. I longed to choose the latter. *He put me on earth for a reason. He will certainly help me achieve that expectation. Why is it so hard to act on that?*

I pondered the two courses. *My life… my choice.* I rose to my feet. Slowly raised my right foot and made my decision. Step number twenty-seven.

UNFINISHED BRIDGES

David F. Hamilton
Santa Clarita, CA

My father called it God's country. My mother called it the edge of the earth. I called it the ninth circle of Hell. In reality, it was Centereach, New York, and a little bit of all three. The State of New York forced my parents to move from their first house, in Massapequa, when the powers that be decided the future growth of Long Island could best be served by building the Seaford-Oyster Bay Expressway through my parents' living room. The State of New York bought their little Cape Cod home for "fair market value," which consisted of enough to pay off their mortgage and leave them $3,000 for a down payment on their next home.

Unfortunately, this was 1961, the age of suburban flight. The white middle class fled New York City in droves, trying to escape the "undesirable elements" that flocked to the city in search of jobs, and their own piece of the American dream. This caused property values in the suburban bedroom communities like Levittown and Massapequa to skyrocket. My parents had no choice but to move farther out on the island, to Suffolk County. Builders had only begun to develop Suffolk County, and they needed to offer a little something extra to entice people to move so far from the city. After all, people still had to work in the city, and the drive from Suffolk County into New York took over an hour each way.

Heatherwood was one of the first housing developments to be built in central Suffolk County, in a little town called Centereach. It featured a golf course and a strip mall that included a Waldbaum's supermarket, a movie theater, a bagel shop, a deli, a pizza place and a drug store. More importantly, my parents could buy a three-bedroom ranch, with a full basement, on a wooded, third of an acre lot, for $11,500. So, we moved to God's country, the edge of the earth, the ninth circle of Hell.

By 1968 Vietnam had taken over the role of the ninth circle of Hell. In fact, in my mind, Centereach had elevated itself to the status of the fifth circle of Purgatory, the circle of the avaricious and prodigal. The land of plenty had become the land of never enough.

I turned up the radio and "Mr. Businessman," Ray Stevens' latest single, blasted from the speakers.

> Itemize the things you covet,
> As you squander through your life,
> Bigger cars, bigger houses,
> Term insurance for your wife.

I sang along, blissfully unaware of the hypocrisy of singing that song as I sped down Nicholls Road in my Dad's 1967 Charger. The 383-cubic-inch V-8 engine, with the four-barrel carburetor and dual exhaust, burned gas at the horrifying rate of eight miles per gallon and blew carbon monoxide into the air like there was no tomorrow. Of course, at that time, I believed in tomorrow. I had just turned sixteen. I was invincible, immortal. Tomorrow was a sure thing, a given. Five hours later, I learned differently.

As I reached the end of Nicholls Road, where it emptied onto Route 25A, I stared up at the bridge. I had driven under this same bridge hundreds of times, and never given it a second thought. That night would be different. That night we would claim this bridge as our own.

It had to be done. We had no choice, really. This was the last weekend of the summer. Monday morning we would all be seniors, proud members of the first graduating class from Ward Melville High School. The class of '69. We had no traditions. The school had only been built in 1966, to accommodate the kids who grew up in Heatherwood and the dozens of other developments that followed. The school needed a tradition. As the first graduating class, the responsibility fell to us.

We conceived a flawless plan. Mark, Todd and I all told our parents the same lie, about having an all-night card game at Dave's summer place in Sound Beach. The games had become regular monthly events lately, so no one questioned the story. The trunk of my car carried all the necessary supplies: a gallon of sunflower yellow paint, a four-inch brush, and a heavy-duty rope my Dad had bought years ago for a Cub Scout tug-of-war.

We arrived at the trestle just after midnight, about five minutes before the last scheduled train passed through. I parked the car on a little dirt path that wound around behind an embankment. I killed the lights and the engine, and turned toward my friends.

"Are we ready?"

"Let's do it," they answered in unison.

We retrieved our supplies, and headed up the embankment, toward history.

As we reached the top, a horn blared. I turned and stared down the tracks at a speck of approaching light as a second blast heralded the train's arrival. The rhythmic clatter drew closer and the light intensified, reflecting off the mist rising from the still-warm earth. The train's light divided the rising steam into mist figures that danced along the rails, arm in arm until the train slammed into them and scattered them to the winds. My gaze followed the red taillights until they disappeared into the distance.

Mark was the lightest of us, so we decided he should be the painter. I tied one end of the rope around my waist, walked across the tracks and leaned against the back wall. Dave threw the other end over the front edge of the trestle, as Mark ran his belt through the handle of the paint can and stuck the handle of the paintbrush in his back pocket. Dave and Todd grabbed hold of the rope as Mark rappelled down the side of the trestle. Mark weighed only about a hundred and fifty pounds, and the three of us had no trouble supporting his weight.

At first, everything went according to plan. Mark had just finished painting

"CLASS OF" in huge yellow letters. He moved to the right, shifted into position to add the "69." Then we heard the sirens. Within seconds, two police cars screamed onto Nicholls Road, sirens wailing and lights flashing.

"Oh, shit!" Dave yelled. "They saw us." Dave and Todd jumped up to see what was happening, and momentarily lost their grip on the rope.

That was all it took. The sudden extra weight pulled me off balance and across the tracks. Dave and Todd tried to grab the rope, but it burned through their hands. I tripped over one of the rails and stumbled forward, finally slamming to a stop as my shoulder banged into the steel wall. I became vaguely aware of the sirens roaring on into the distance. They hadn't seen us after all. Thank God. I felt around my waist, momentarily relieved that the rope was still tied tight. Then it hit me. There was no weight on the other end.

"Oh my God," I said, and jumped up. Dave and Todd already stared over the edge.

Mark lay in a heap on the asphalt below. Dave and Todd turned and ran down the embankment, but I just stood there, staring down at Mark's crumpled body.

Somehow, I just knew.

I hadn't visited the old neighborhood in twenty-five years. I dropped out of college in 1976, and took a job as a manager trainee for a large sporting goods manufacturer. In 1983, they offered me a promotion to manage their national distribution center in Greensboro, North Carolina, and I jumped at the chance to get off Long Island. I would never have come back at all if my daughter hadn't wanted to be a doctor. SUNY at Stony Brook had earned a reputation as one of the best teaching hospitals in the country, and Karen insisted on doing her internship there. I dropped her off for her final interview, and decided to drive around the old stomping grounds while I waited. Nothing much had changed. Of course, there were more traffic lights on the roads, and the requisite malls and multiplexes had been built to accommodate Suffolk County's burgeoning population, but it still felt the same. It remained the kind of place where people didn't lock their doors at night, and didn't worry whether the Good Humor man's crisp white uniform hid a child molester. After a few hours, I turned onto Nicholls Road, heading back toward the university, and there it stood.

The bridge. I stared up at the trestle and wondered how many times it had been painted over the last forty years. The present coat of paint looked fresh, its battleship gray finish unblemished by rust or graffiti. I imagined a series of canary yellow letters forming on the gray panels, spelling out the words "CLASS OF." I shook my head. We had never finished the bridge, never established our tradition.

Maybe that was our tradition. Maybe that was the legacy of my generation, a legacy of never finishing what we started, of short-lived passions and unfulfilled dreams, of unfinished bridges. We wanted our generation remembered as the generation of peace and love, of ecology and civil rights. We dreamed of changing the world. Forty years later war rages in the Middle East. Divorce rates and teenage pregnancy have risen to all-time highs. We continue to consume our natural resources with reckless abandon. Men and women still judge each other, as Dr. King feared, by the color of their skin, or their gender, or religion, rather than the contents of their characters.

I had certainly constructed enough unfinished bridges in my own life: my first marriage, my education, and the half-written novel gathering dust in a desk drawer. The trestle had simply been the first of many, and as the first, it seemed to have a causal relationship to all the rest. Maybe if we had just finished that bridge, I could've found the strength to stick it out when my marriage foundered, to put in the time and get my degree, to fight my way through writer's block. It seemed ridiculous, but that stupid bridge had become the symbol for all the failures in my life.

Karen aced her interview. I took her out to dinner to celebrate, but I wasn't very good company. My mind wandered elsewhere, elsewhen.

That night I made a decision. Three months later, when I brought Karen back to begin her internship, I carried it out.

It was cold up on the trestle. The rope I "borrowed" from the marina hung wet and heavy over my shoulder. I never should have tried to do this alone. I took a screwdriver from my back pocket and pried the lid off the can of sunflower paint cradled between my knees. I looked down at the horrendous, garish yellow, a perfect choice to stand out against the steel gray of the bridge.

A horn blared. I turned and stared down the tracks at a speck of approaching light as a second blast heralded the train's arrival. The rhythmic clatter drew closer and the light intensified, reflecting off the mist rising from the still-warm earth. The train's light divided the rising steam into mist figures that danced along the rails. There were three. They had no discernible shape, but I sensed who had joined me — Dave, Todd, and Mark. The spectres walked along the tracks, arm in arm until the train slammed into them, and scattered them to the winds.

My gaze followed the red taillights until they disappeared into the distance. I secured one end of the rope around a cement pylon and tossed the other end over the edge of the trestle. I stared back across the tracks and saw a single mist figure reassemble and move toward me. It was Mark, impossibly, fantastically, Mark. He wore the same faded jeans and Doors tee shirt he did the last time I saw him. He laughed, a hollow, ethereal chuckle.

I stared blankly, my emotions a slide projector on fast-forward. Confusion. Guilt. Elation. Sorrow. Friendship. Loss. Depression. Mark hovered, as insubstantial as his laugh. I saw through him, saw the mist rising on the other side of the tracks behind him. Tears gathered, refusing to stay in the corners of my eyes. They overflowed and raced down my cheeks in a mad dash for my chin. I knew he wasn't real. He was a trick of the light, or the dark, or the mist, or my guilt. I ran toward Mark's apparition, threw my arms around him, grabbed only mist and my own cold, damp shoulders.

I was losing it, but I knew that if I could just finish this, everything would be okay. I ran my belt through the handle of the paint can, held the brush between clenched teeth, and lowered myself over the side. My knees and elbows chafed as they banged and scraped along the metal wall. The coarse mooring rope burned my hands as I descended. Finally, my feet felt the four-inch ledge at the base of the trestle. I angled my feet to get as firm a footing as possible, and then coiled my right arm through the rope, leaving my left hand free to paint.

The first few letters presented no problem. I loosened my grip a little and let out about another foot or two of rope, and then inched my way to the right. My right foot slipped and I fell back. My own weight snapped the rope taut, and nearly yanked my arm out of its socket. Pain blurred my vision for a few seconds, but I regained my foothold and pulled myself back into position.

When I finished writing "CLASS OF," shivers of terror coursed through my body. I was afraid to look down, afraid I'd see Mark's body sprawled on the black asphalt. I was afraid to look up, fearing I'd see the terrified faces of Dave and Todd staring down at me. I froze, stared straight ahead at the cold grayness of the bridge. I felt a slight tug on the rope from above, summoned all my courage, and looked up. I was surprised to see not Todd and Dave staring down at me, but Mark.

"You disappointed me more than anyone," he said, pointing a mist finger at me.

"I'm sorry," I said. "I tried to hold you. I just—"

"Not that, you idiot!" Mark's rage turned the ethereal voice into a keening howl.

I managed only a weak reply. "We were friends. Best friends."

"That's the point," Mark said. "I didn't expect as much from the others." He shook his head. "What happened to you, man? You never finished anything in your life."

"That's not fair," I replied weakly.

"Oh, please, don't give me that crap. You know what's not fair? It's not fair that I'm dead, and you're alive, and you've wasted the last forty years."

I couldn't respond.

Mark sneered down at me. "How's that novel coming?"

Silence.

"When did you finish college?"

Silence.

"When was the last time you spoke to Drusilla?"

Forty years of buried feelings erupted with a fury I didn't know was in me. "It's your fault!" I screamed at him. "You deserted me. I had my shit together. I knew what I wanted. When you died, everything fell apart, and I hated you for it."

"Fuck you!" Mark wrapped misty fingers around the shimmering hilt of a knife. He pulled the blade. It flickered in the shadows as if forged from shards of moonlight. "That's why you're the worst, man. You blame everything that's screwed up in your life on me. You can't take responsibility for your own failure. Well, I'm not taking it anymore. I'm not guilty, you hear me? Not fucking guilty! You never finished anything in your whole life!" My old friend drew back and cut the rope with his glimmering blade, shouting, "And you're not going to finish this bridge!"

I fell. Blackness surrounded me, the wind whistled in my ears.

SNAP!

Blinding pain engulfed me. I lay dying on the asphalt, in the exact spot Mark had died forty years earlier. I was cold, and something wet soaked into my pants and shirt.

No, I was not on the ground. I could sense my feet dangling in mid-air. The snap I'd heard came from the rope, and the pain from a dislocated shoulder. I looked up. Mark's ghostly apparition had vanished. The rope wasn't cut. Somehow, I'd managed to hang on despite my dislocated shoulder. The paintbrush was still in my left hand. The gallon can still dangled from my belt, although at least half of it had sloshed out all over my clothes. I wrapped my legs around the rope, put the brush handle between my teeth, pulled myself up, each tug on the rope birthing new spasms of pain.

When I reached the spot where I had been painting, I wanted to keep going, to pull myself back to the top and go home. The pain was excruciating, and emanated in waves to every part of my body. I needed a doctor. I needed warmth. I needed sleep. I needed to put this nightmare of dead friends and unfinished bridges behind me.

No, not this time. I regained a foothold and took the brush in my left hand, as my right shoulder threw out fresh lightning bolts of pain in all directions. Through the flashes of pain and memory, an idea formed. It was never too late to start a tradition. I dipped the brush into the remaining paint.

Karen said the sling could come off in about two weeks. I left the hospital with a dull ache in my shoulder, but overall, feeling better than I had in years. A few days later, I drove down to the trestle. There was a road crew there, inspecting my artwork. I pulled over onto the little dirt path where I had hidden the car three nights, and forty years, before, and then got out and walked over to the crew chief.

"What's going on?" I asked.

"Kids," he said, shaking his head. "Bunch of kids from the high school must've thought it would be cool to paint the trestle."

"No kidding?"

"Waste of time, though," he said. "Soon as the city council found out about it, they sent us out here to cover it up. I just hope this doesn't become a regular thing."

"You never know," I said, and then watched as a boom truck raised a worker with a can of battleship gray paint toward the trestle.

I walked back a few paces and turned to take a last look at my handiwork before it was covered forever:

CLASS OF 2008.

I wondered if the graduating seniors would ever know that it was not one of their own who had painted the bridge. I wondered if the class of 2009 would carry on the tradition. I wondered if Mark was proud of me.

It didn't matter. The tradition had been started. The class of '69 had finally paid its debt to history. My bridge had finally been finished. Perhaps it would be the first of many.

HARD STOP

Jamie Rotham
Columbus, OH

My birthday balloon is still here. Floating above me, swaying in an artificial breeze. The Mylar is holding the helium in place and I've decided to leave it up as long as possible. No reason. Maybe because it makes me smile.

Stop. Reboot.

The sun is hitting the glass on the window and struggling to pierce the curtains that do nothing but look tacky on the door to the patio to which we're not allowed to venture.

System check.

I WANT TO GO HOME.

Sorry… didn't mean to shout. Just happened. Just popped out. I do want to go home though… well, maybe not home. More like somewhere. On a trip. I don't know. But being at work today feels torturous. And while there is many an important thing happening at my office today, each feels small and finite. Total rubbish. It feels… this isn't how I want to spend the rest of my life.

Sitting at a desk doing somebody else's planning and thinking. Taking the little creative reserve I have left and pouring it into every work-related project I have and thus leaving nothing but a withered husk where my creativity once flourished.

I feel dry.

Inside.

Cold. Like the Antarctic desert. My latest script sits alone on some disk space, whimpering at me, asking why I don't talk to it anymore. Why I avoid its stares and change the subject when someone asks me about it.

I should have skipped work today. Yes, there's a huge work group thing today. Yes, we're all supposed to be there. Yes, it would've really bit me in the ass to call in "sick." But fuck it. Yes. Fuck it. There's a time for frakin' and a time for fuckin' and right now I feel like being a little more vulgar than my usual less vulgar self.

And for that I cannot apologize. I should've called up my boss, told her I couldn't make it, and taken a friend up on his roadtrip offer. You can't live forever.

Here's the kick in the crotch. I actually like my job. How much more unbearable is this feeling for those who hate theirs? I sit here today and want to be anywhere else. I want to sit at a bar upstate and share a beer with my best friend. I want to go to a non-commercialized coffee shop where the people are artists, not pretenders, and write a scene of my script today. I want to have lunch with my mother. I want to stand at the edge of the world and sound my barbaric yawp.

Not the squeak of a crushed spirit. The pathetic whimpering of a man trudging through existence.

Error. Reboot.

More thoughts I do not wish to share in public forum. I don't like secrets. But I understand the need for them. And these aren't secrets so much as just my private musings… they are for me. Some might be fit for sharing down the road, but right now, they are mine.

I lie to my coworkers. They ask me how I am and I tell them that I'm well or that I can't complain. "Can't complain?" Seriously? Yes. Yes I can. Legitimately? Probably not. But in the grand scheme… I'm not fine at work. Good job, but it's eating my soul. I'm constantly creating here and that takes away what I might create at home. And yes, I work on my own stuff as much as I can. But lunches and breaks are ill substitute for the freedom of waking up, slinging the Blackbird over my shoulder, and heading out to write.

To see. To observe. To love. To live.

Here in the confines of these old walls, that does not happen. We all make our own personal Hell. My high school band director taught me that. It's unfortunate that I'm good at making things happen.

System check. Defragmentation.

I have a meeting in four minutes that I don't want to attend. I want to walk outside, get in my car, and drive to Lake Erie. Not even to jump in. Heck, I'll take a day at a local lake. I want to sit on the water in the crisp air today. I want to write something that isn't about selling the message or the brand.

I should be on my way upstate right now. I don't do things like that. And that's responsible. I know that. It's also killing me.

You'd think I would've learned something in college. Maybe just something. Like how sometimes it's okay to fall down. It's okay to take the leap and not make it. It's not the end of the world to fail and to admit it. It's okay.

Sometimes crashing and burning creates the ashes from which a person rises anew. I haven't crashed yet. But I feel like I'm in the steep dive, hands pulling up on the stick as best I can. And every day that I walk in here, or do anything antithetical to me becoming a writer, I get a little closer to the impact crater.

Seventeen noises. Typing, air circulation, coworker chatter, construction nearby, birds chirping, my own breath, a podcast wafts through the air, phones ringing… and more and more and more in the wild cacophony that echoes about me here and follows me outside and everywhere I go.

So many thoughts. So many things to do. E-mails I don't want to read. Phone calls I don't want to take. Nail me down an' whip me. The vegetables will rot. Shit needs cleaned.

So much happening. So much going to happen. Still life moving. That's mine. Can't have it.

Going to change. Going to be hard. Caffeine is my drug of choice. Off the Coke. Not withdrawal of commercialized addiction. Clarity. The black hole is not the portal.

Ancient bricks doth crumble and statues topple. To sands stretched far. Out out brief candle.

Talking nonsense.

Never ceasing. Never changing. All the din. The lion roars. The girl cries.

Wind blows across my face and I feel it calming me. Waves crash. Like thunder. The thunder cliffs. Goodbye Northman. Can't change it. No take-backs. Uh-uh, that wouldn't be fair, old sport.

Interaction at its lowest point. A hollow fuck, a meaningful kiss. Confusion on the Orient Express. The rain comes down. Like grace. It's washed away.

The boss is talking. I smile. Espresso punches me. A tic-tac. Not happening. Confusion. Derailment. Interruption of the flow. Can't stop the—

Hard stop.

Reboot.

System check.

It's going to be okay.

MOONFLOWERS

Kathleen Olive Palmer
Fort Lauderdale, FL

In the afternoon sun
day becomes night

Moonflowers
at peace with the world
disappear

strong vines
climbing the sky

Under the hidden moon
a silent blossoming
of angels

the deep night dreams
we seek

BULL-VAULTING

Annabelle Moseley
Dix Hills, NY

I. The Hunt

You're on its trail, like Theseus; you hunt
a minotaur. Half-man, half-bull, your beast
of transformation— tragedy. A grunt
from its huge body (echoing, released
from some dark place) resounds. You think of her—
she gave you tethered thread to find your way
back, new birth-cord. (Her pretty face blurs
in your thoughts now, down in this maze where day
has never shone.) You meet the monster, face
its cattle-skull, horns sharpened, muscled flesh
gleaming with sweat and stained with a fresh trace
of blood. You're battle-wild, the air a mesh
of fear and rage. Courage and fists, alike,
both rising up. And so, you move and strike.

II. The Kill

Painted on cave walls of your former lives—
(and all within your one life) primal forms,
scratched, bruised, transform their arms to wings. The drives
of animal things— fierce, fleeting as storms
is what propels the dance to find its way—
through this labyrinth of judgment, anger, blame,
sorrow, grief, violence. And any day,
a friend may weaken. They may curse your name,
gossip or lie. All this is nothing to
the sufferings you've seen, the ones you've lost—
to death and to the world. Here's what to do.
You'll vault over the monster, cry out, tossed,
then turn and strike, and knock it flat.   Reborn,
stand up. Bow to the beast that made you mourn.

FALLING AWAY

Robert Taylor
Akron, OH

SCENE ONE--THE MCCARTHY HOUSEHOLD LIVING ROOM

A single light bathes the dark stage, revealing JEREMY, a good looking young man, 23 years of age. He is pacing back and forth across the stage, a small engagement ring box in his left hand, open. The light on the stage gradually rises, revealing a well-dressed living room of an upper-middle-class family home, a staircase near the back of the stage leading to an unseen second floor. JEREMY continues to stare at the ring in the box as he paces.

MARK, JEREMY'S father, a handsome man in his early fifties, enters. JEREMY does not acknowledge him.

MARK
Really, son? It's not going to flinch no matter how much you stare it down.

(JEREMY pauses, looks up and pulls the ring from the box. He approaches MARK with the ring outstretched in his hand.)

JEREMY
The ring has imperfections. There are two tiny scratches on the gold band here... and here. And one of these things that holds onto the diamond... what's it called?

MARK
The diamondy-holdy-thingy.

JEREMY
The diamondy-holdy thingy is a little warped here. Do you see it?

MARK
No.

JEREMY
Yes you do. Right here.

(JEREMY holds the ring two inches from MARK'S left eyeball.)

MARK

I really don't. And if you shove that thing any closer I'm going to use that diamond to adorn the eye patch I'm going to buy.

> (JEREMY laughs feebly before turning and beginning to inspect the ring again.)

MARK (CONT'D)

Look, I know you want everything to be absolutely perfect.

JEREMY

(Not listening)

I just want everything to be perfect for her, dad. And even if I didn't, everything would have to be absolutely perfect or Iris would kill me.

MARK

Trust me, Jeremy. Imperfections are...oh Lord...grapefruit. Kiwi.

> (No reaction.)

MARK (CONT'D)

Probably one of those fake diamonds that you used to create when you were a kid and put those rocks in that water and then shook and...

JEREMY

I did NOT play with those.

MARK

I specifically remember buying one.

JEREMY

For Mom?

MARK

However cheap I may be, I would never give my wife plastic jewelry. It's semi-precious or bust.

JEREMY

What about her engagement ring?

MARK

Cracker Jack box.

JEREMY

Huh?

MARK

You make a pop culture reference and the dinner table collectively chokes on their spaghetti because they are laughing so hard. I make a pop culture reference and am met with "huhs" and "oh pleases."

(JEREMY has already begun to inspect the ring again.)

MARK (CONT'D)

Look. You want a completely perfect proposal, go for it. But remember, it's the quirky mistakes that make the proposal memorable. Proposing to your future wife on the big screen at Jacob's Field is all well and good, but having the stadium collectively "boo" her because she is wearing a t-shirt supporting the opposing team... now that is what I call a memory. Or having her choke on the ring at the bottom of the champagne glass. Or having her fall on the ice because she was too busy looking at her ring to remember she was on ice skates, or...

JEREMY

Why do you want Iris to suffer, dad?

MARK

Oh yeah, I forgot you loved her and all.

JEREMY

Do you think I should take it back?

MARK

The ring?

JEREMY

The ring.

MARK

Because of two tiny scratches and the diamondy-holdy-thingie?

JEREMY

Yes.

MARK

No.

JEREMY

Yes.

MARK

Jer, how long have you been inspecting that ring? By the tread marks on the carpet I would say at least an hour.

JEREMY

Or four.

MARK

Did you take a break for *The View*?

JEREMY

I don't watch *The View*.

MARK

You are right. You don't watch *The View*. You watch *The Tyra Banks Show* and I wanted the embarrassment to be less for you, so I tell everyone you watch *The View*.

JEREMY

You tell everyone about my late-morning television viewing habits?

MARK

No. I lie about it so you don't embarrass the family.

JEREMY

Oy. No, I did not watch *The View* or *Tyra* or anything else this morning.

MARK

Then how do you know that is actually two tiny scratches and... I can't be bothered to say that name again... when it could just be that your eyes are too tired to see anything but?

JEREMY

Because I...

MARK

I made breakfast. Now go grab your bowl and watch the *Tyra* that I helpfully TiVo'd.

(MARK snatches the ring from JEREMY, places it back in its box and puts it in his pocket.)

JEREMY

Fine. When will I get it back?

MARK

After you forget and think it's only one imperfection and a possible problem with the diamondy-holdy-thingy.

JEREMY

Was *Tyra* new?

MARK

Yes. Maybe. I wouldn't know.

(JESSICA, MARK'S wife and JEREMY'S mother, enters in a robe with her hair astrew. She is just a bit younger than her husband, and stunningly pretty for her age.)

JESSICA

Good morning, all.

MARK

Morning, dear.

JEREMY

Hello.

MARK

Our son has been pacing our carpet for four hours inspecting the engagement ring he intends to give Iris. He didn't even have the courtesy to grind a track into his own apartment.

JESSICA

I like it when he's here.

(A beat.)

MARK

I made cereal, dear wife of mine, for you and our son.

JEREMY

How exactly do you MAKE cereal, Dad?

MARK

If I would have made omelets you would have asked the exact same question.

(JEREMY exits to the kitchen.)

MARK

So how was your evening, my dear wife?

JESSICA

You need to learn that three dry martinis for me is too much.

(JESSICA walks to MARK and leans against him, placing her head on his shoulder.)

MARK

I like it when your left eyelid starts speaking to me in Morse code.

JESSICA

Do you have to work today?

MARK

Not until four.

JESSICA

Let's go back to bed.

SCENE TWO—INT. JEREMY'S APARTMENT, LATER THAT DAY

The apartment is a small studio apartment, with a daybed doubling as a couch and a small dining area stage right, where we find IRIS setting the table. JEREMY enters.

JEREMY

Hello, dear girl.

(JEREMY crosses stage and kisses IRIS affectionately.)

IRIS

I'm totally and completely freaking out here.

JEREMY

What?

IRIS

Do you know that your oven stops working if you put it above two-hundred-and-seventy-five degrees? And while that may be fine for the baking of Bagel Bites and Pizza Rolls, how am I supposed to cook you a five-course masterpiece with low heat, cracked casserole dishes and no big spoons!

JEREMY

Iris, you are as beautiful as the flower that acts as your namesake…

IRIS

Oy, that clause always ends with a pat on the head about my borderline OCD.

JEREMY

Borderline?
    (Laughs)

    (IRIS pouts.)

JEREMY (CONT'D)

Now come on, dear. You know I love every single thing about you, from your propensity to speak along during musicals but not sing during musical numbers to that little unguarded smile that you only make once or twice a week when you think no one is looking.

(IRIS smiles despite herself.)

JEREMY (CONT'D)

Nope. Not that one.

(IRIS frowns.)

JEREMY (CONT'D)

But I gave you the key to my apartment to come in whenever you like and surprise me and love me and hold me--not worry about the fact that there are no big spoons and that my casserole dish is cracked.

IRIS

Where were you, anyway?

JEREMY

I went home for a few hours.

IRIS

Oh.

JEREMY

Exactly.

IRIS

Was she there?

JEREMY

Yes, she was.

IRIS

And did you talk to her?

JEREMY

Barely.

(JEREMY crosses stage left.)

JEREMY

In the way in which one could tell I was avoiding it.

IRIS

So in the last three weeks she hasn't even tried talking to you or telling you—well—anything about what happened?

JEREMY

Apparently I'm not worth the time. I know that I need to talk to her... and then talk to him... but...

(IRIS crosses to join JEREMY. They sit together.)

IRIS

Go ahead.

JEREMY

At first I was just mad. Mad that my mother could throw away everything that was so important to her for twenty-seven years and just sleep with another man. Who knows how long she's been sleeping with him, or if she's stopped, or if she intends to stop, or if she is going to leave Dad, or anything. And I couldn't bring myself to talk to her because it just hurt too much...oh so much. Just thinking of her screaming that name... Boyd... it makes me sick.

But now it's completely different. Whereas before all I could do was be mad at her, now I'm mad at myself. I look at my father there, just standing there and thinking everything is fine, just fine. That his life isn't about to be ruined. And I'm too much of a coward to tell him. Or talk to her. Or yell. Or do anything.

IRIS

I know you've always been closer with your father than your mother, Jer...

JEREMY

It's not just that though, Iris. I loved my mother as much as I possibly could, it just hurts me in ways you don't yet understand, and I'm not sure you can.

IRIS

Try me.

(IRIS wraps her hands around JEREMY'S chest and places her head on his shoulder.)

JEREMY

It's just...

IRIS

Don't make me pull out the pookie-bear comments.

JEREMY

I talk adultery and you talk pookie-bear. Fitting.

IRIS

You know you can trust me, my dear.

JEREMY

But right here? Right now? With the spoons and the imperfections and the cracked casserole dishes and everything?

IRIS

I haven't the slightest…

JEREMY

Iris, is the timer going to go off in the next—oh—let's say five minutes?

IRIS

No, why?

JEREMY

And you aren't expecting any deliveries?

IRIS

Is it okay that I am confused?

JEREMY

And your cell phone is set to vibrate right now, right?

IRIS

No, off.

JEREMY

I love you! Oh my God, I love people who aren't afraid to put their cell phone into the off position and still feel comfortable with themselves.

IRIS

Oh I know. People think they seem popular when their cell phones go off, and all they really are is an annoyance…

JEREMY

And vibrating cell phones are just as bad as having the ringer on full blast.

IRIS

I know! Whenever that vibrating noise or the phone just plain goes off in a theater I just wish they would pause the movie or the actors would stop acting and the audience would just pounce on the person.

                              JEREMY
I know!

                               IRIS
We're babbling.

                              JEREMY
I'm babbling?

                               IRIS
Both of us.

                              JEREMY
I'm nervous.

                               IRIS
Why are you nervous?

                              JEREMY
Because since I don't have a ring I'm not sure whether I should get down on
one knee or not.

                               IRIS
Ohmigawd Ohmigawd Ohmigawd!

        (IRIS stands up and begins to jump around the room, leaving a
    dumbfounded, yet smiling, JEREMY still sitting down. IRIS finally calms
    down for a moment and runs back to JEREMY.)

                          IRIS (CONT'D)
Ohmigawd yes yes YES!

                              JEREMY
Well, I haven't asked it yet.

                               IRIS
Well, wait until you have a ring until you ask!

        (A pause.)

                          IRIS (CONT'D)
And why don't you have it yet anyway?

                              JEREMY
Uh, honey... I bought it, I did. But dad ring-napped it.

IRIS

Why don't you make a whole big spiel of it tonight at dinner at your parents' house?

JEREMY

Dinner?

IRIS

Honey, I love you, but I want my ring.

JEREMY

What about the awkwardness that is sure to ensue?

IRIS

Me? Be awkward? I can totally cover up any awkwardness with my talking! Remember the great salad dressing debate of '06?

JEREMY

I still think ranch dressing is better served lukewarm.

IRIS

But honey, if you aren't up for it, I completely understand. And we can have dinner out of the chipped casserole dish and be more than happy here. Besides, we just got engaged.

(IRIS begins to kiss JEREMY'S neck as she rubs his chest.)

IRIS (CONT'D)

It's time to celebrate.
(Jeremy kisses her back before pulling away and standing.)

JEREMY

No Iris, you are right. You should have your ring and I should be able to walk into that house without being nervous or afraid and put it on your beautiful finger. I'm calling Dad and we are going over there in one half-hour's time… and what we do during that half-hour is completely up to you.

(JEREMY winks and walks to the phone.)

SCENE THREE—THE MCCARTHY KITCHEN—ALMOST CONTINUOUS

The kitchen is very well put together, full of huge metal appliances and antiseptic lighting. MARK is on the phone with JEREMY as JESSICA pretends to do busywork while listening intently to the conversation.

MARK

Alright, see you soon. Love to Iris.

(MARK hangs up the phone.)

MARK (CONT'D)

Well, Jeremy and Iris are coming for dinner, and he hinted that he most definitely wants the engagement ring back sooner rather than later. What were you making?

(JESSICA is quiet, her mind elsewhere.)

MARK (CONT'D)

Jess?

JESSICA

Oh, I'm sorry. What did you say?

MARK

Jeremy and Iris are coming for dinner. What are we having and do you need help?

JESSICA

Oh, uh, spaghetti and meatballs with garlic toast. Let me think... yes... yes, we have enough ingredients to go around for everyone. I'll get to it.

MARK

Think we should invite Cameron? Vending machine food and fast food joints have to get old at some point, don't they?

JESSICA

I miss her too, Mark. But we probably should wait until she is ready to come home for the first time before begging her to.

MARK

But it's been almost a week! And the college is only 20 minutes away, and that gives me nine more to talk you into letting our baby girl...

JESSICA

Freshman in college baby girl.

MARK

... partake in a home-cooked meal made with loving care and attention by her wonderful, not to mention beautiful, mother.
    (JESSICA is silent.)

MARK (CONT'D)

Pretty please? I'll buy you candy and flowers and make sure when I buy the flowers that they are the perfect pink/purple gerbera daisies that you love so dearly. I'll buy you so many that you can just rip off the petals and literally bathe in gerbera daisy petals.

(JESSICA remains a bit aloof as she moves to the refrigerator and the cabinets to begin preparing dinner.)

JESSICA

I miss her too, but we promised to wait until she called home wanting to come home, simple as that. And don't try any more of your witty witticisms on me, Mr. Man. My mind will become all flustered and I'll burn the sauce while trying to sort through what you just said to me. It would be completely different if she simply called and…

(The phone rings.)

MARK

You don't think that this is the one time in our lives when a coincidence timed this perfectly…

(The phone rings again.)

MARK (CONT'D)

… is happening, do you? That would just be… ridiculous.

(MARK picks up the phone.)

MARK (CONT'D)

Hello?

CAMERON (O.S.)

Daddy!

(MARK'S mouth drops and he mouths "It's her!" at JESSICA.)

MARK

How is my beautiful baby girl doing this bright and dandy day?

CAMERON (O.S.)

Somewhat bright and somewhat dandy. I would be brighter and dandier if I was in the arms of my loving family and a working washing machine that doesn't rob me of quarters I would much rather use on vending machines.

MARK

You want to come home?

CAMERON (O.S.)

I was planning on it. In fact I'm already here and overheard your conversation from the living room.

(CAMERON enters the kitchen and is immediately pounced upon by her parents.)

JESSICA

Welcome home!

MARK

That was a dirty, dirty mind game you were playing on your parents! Now tell us, did you really come home for us or because of the dirty laundry?

CAMERON

Dad!

JESSICA

Now leave our daughter alone, Mark. Now Cam, do you want to rest, relax and watch your recorded shows or help me with dinner? I need to know now because I am in complete and utter danger of falling madly behind in making it.

CAMERON

You want me on garlic bread duty or pasta duty? I'm leaving the sauce in your hands.

JESSICA

Garlic bread.

CAMERON

On it.

JESSICA

And you, husband-'o-mine, you go bring in the heaps of clothing that somehow Cameron must have amassed in one week and start a load downstairs, pronto.

MARK

As you wish.

(MARK exits. JESSICA and CAMERON get to work on their various tasks.)

JESSICA

So…

CAMERON
(After a brief pause)
It was okay. Fine. A fine-ish okay.

JESSICA
I know it's a bit of a big transition, what with only one or two classes a day and all that time on your hands that you never had before.

CAMERON
I mean, I knew it would be a new experience and something I needed to get adjusted to… but I feel very isolated up there.

JESSICA
Your friends are a short drive away.

CAMERON
I know, I know. But I was so used to seeing everyone every day of my life and keeping my friends that way, and now I'm sitting in my dorm room for four hours straight gorging on cookies and when I do call them I then sit by the phone pretending to watch TV and do my readings and my homework when all I want to do is have them call me back or call them again, but if I do then I feel like a stalker… and I don't know. It's hard.

JESSICA
I understand. You know, Cam, that the reason most people say that you make your best friends, the ones that really last, in college is because you do. Now I know you had an amazing group of friends in high school…

CAMERON
Then why won't they call me back, mom?

JESSICA
…but college is different. You can't expect to hang on to the same people forever. Now who have you talked to up there?

CAMERON
Alyssa called me back and we got lunch. So did Meghan.

JESSICA
What about that boy Ryan?

CAMERON
No.

JESSICA
Honey, please believe me when I tell you that the best possible thing you can do right now is to leave the cell phone alone in your dorm room for one whole

day and take a walk around campus. Look at the places you can visit and talk to people. Go to the library and check out a book. Do *some*thing with your day.

CAMERON

Or else my cookie gorging will cause me to force you to buy me an entirely new wardrobe.

JEREMY (O.S.)

Hello?

CAMERON

Jeremy is here!?

(CAMERON gets up to run into the living room but hesitates for a moment.)

JESSICA

Go ahead, dear. I'll finish the food while you…

(JEREMY and IRIS walk into the kitchen before JESSICA can finish. CAMERON embraces JEREMY before letting go and hugging IRIS. JEREMY stares at his mother for a beat before she looks away to put the garlic bread into the oven.)

JESSICA

Food will be ready in five minutes. Iris dear, do you want to taste the sauce?

IRIS

No, thank you.

JESSICA

Oh. Uh, how about you, Cam?

(CAMERON moves and takes a spoonful of the sauce, nodding at her mother.)

CAMERON

Wonderful.

JESSICA

Excellent. Can you dump the pasta into the strainer while I check on the garlic bread?

JEREMY

So, my dear sweet sister, how is college?

(CAMERON does as her mother tells her.)

CAMERON

Oh, you know. This and that. I had one whole class today before I came home and I'm SO tired.

JESSICA

Jeremy, dear...

JEREMY

Mother.

(JESSICA looks up to confront JEREMY, but MARK enters.)

MARK

Well, look who showed back up.

(Mark hugs his son and then kisses IRIS on the cheek.)

JESSICA

Mark, will you set the table?

MARK

Of course.

IRIS

I'll help. Cameron, dear, I know you must have at least one story from your first week.

(IRIS cuts MARK off from getting to the drawer.)

CAMERON

Well, nothing completely and totally major that would make its way into my autobiography, I'm sure. The campus is nice and hilly and just a little bit depressing because I just know it's going to be hell to walk through in the winter. And in class, people actually, like, raise their hands and stuff in order to be called on instead of just sinking in their seats and doing that half-awake/ half-asleep thing that everyone perfected perfectly in high school, and that was a little bit of a shocker for me, but the teachers seem totally into the attention they are getting and they are pretty nice, except for my biology teacher, who is a woman but I think might secretly be a man, which would make the whole aspect of him teaching biology oh-so-ironic.

JEREMY
(quietly, to Mark)

I need that ring, Dad.

MARK

Of course, son. Do you remember what imperfections there were on it this morning?

JEREMY

No idea.

MARK

You are either humoring me, and humoring me well, or actually have forgotten. Either way, here you go.

> (MARK produces the ring and subtly hands it to JEREMY so that IRIS does not see.)

JESSICA

Alrighty, everyone. Table is set, pasta is strained, bread is done and sauce is warm. Shall we eat?

MARK

We shall, my dear.

IRIS
(quietly, to JEREMY)

You get it?

JEREMY

I got it.

IRIS

Cha ching!

> (The group sits at their dinner table while JESSICA makes plates of food and passes them out.)

CAMERON

What about you, Mom and D ad? How was your first whole week without either Jer or me in the house?

MARK

Best sleep in over twenty years. Biggest portions of breakfast and dinner in over twenty years. And we get control of the remote every night. I think it's safe to say we don't miss you at all.

JESSICA

Please, Mark. We missed you desperately, both of us. The house gets so... quiet without two children running around.

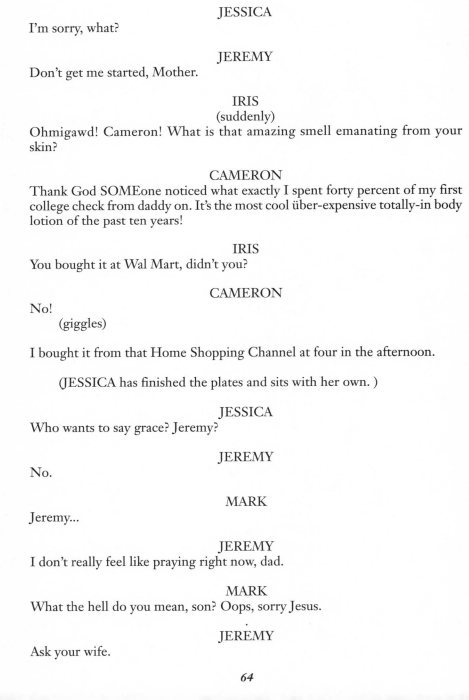

JEREMY

Quiet?

JESSICA

I'm sorry, what?

JEREMY

Don't get me started, Mother.

IRIS
(suddenly)
Ohmigawd! Cameron! What is that amazing smell emanating from your skin?

CAMERON

Thank God SOMEone noticed what exactly I spent forty percent of my first college check from daddy on. It's the most cool über-expensive totally-in body lotion of the past ten years!

IRIS

You bought it at Wal Mart, didn't you?

CAMERON

No!
    (giggles)

I bought it from that Home Shopping Channel at four in the afternoon.

(JESSICA has finished the plates and sits with her own.)

JESSICA

Who wants to say grace? Jeremy?

JEREMY

No.

MARK

Jeremy...

JEREMY

I don't really feel like praying right now, dad.

MARK

What the hell do you mean, son? Oops, sorry Jesus.

JEREMY

Ask your wife.

Your mother.

JEREMY

Your wife.

MARK

Jessica, what does he...

IRIS

Jeremy and I are engaged!

CAMERON

What?

IRIS

Engaged! All he has to do is give me the ring his father was holding hostage, hopefully not because he hates me.
(Laughs)

CAMERON

Seriously?

IRIS

Seriously.

CAMERON

No, seriously? Jer?

JEREMY

Yeah...

CAMERON

Holy shit!

IRIS

Holy shit!

MARK

I was not holding the ring hostage from you, dear. Merely from my son and his ever-growing OCD.

IRIS

Actually, chances are his OCD is merely my OCD disguised as him caring about imperfections in the ring. Am I right?

(JEREMY doesn't answer; he's staring at his mother.)

IRIS (CONT'D)

Jeremy?

CAMERON

That is so very sweet. Am I too old to be the flower girl?

IRIS

Well, I actually thinking maid of honor, but I wanted to ask you quietly when we were in a room alone so you could turn it down if you wanted. Whoops.

JEREMY

Mother, could I see you for a minute in the other room?

JESSICA

Honey, we are celebrating...

JEREMY

Now.

(JESSICA gets up and begins to follow JEREMY into the living room.)

IRIS
(Loudly as possible)

So anyway, I want lilies for my wedding because, as pretty as it would be to have irises since that is my name and all, and haven't you ever wondered if the plural for iris was iris' or iris's or iris's's' or what? Haha! Anyway, that would be totally a cliché and the last thing we need at a wedding, in my humble opinion, which since I'm the bride is the only opinion that counts, is for me to be even more of a cliché than I normally would be, so I'm thinking lilies, or even daisies as...

JEREMY (O.S.)

You know it, mother, you know it!

CAMERON

Dad, what's going on?

JESSICA (O.S.)

You have no fucking idea what you are talking about.

MARK

What's going on is my son and my wife have not been talking and making excuses about why they aren't.

CAMERON

Why?

Chances are I'm about to find out.

(MARK begins to get up from the table and IRIS moves to stop him panicking.)

IRIS

Please, don't.

CAMERON

Go, Dad.

(There is a crash in the living room, followed by JESSICA screaming and running into the kitchen.)

JESSICA

Mark! Mark! He's on the floor! He's shaking! I don't know what to do!

(All members of the table race toward the living room door. The stage is suddenly bathed in black.)

AMERICAN SALESMAN

Charles C. Nwachukwu
Austin, TX

EXT. FAIRFAX LANE – DAY

The picture-perfect image of suburbia: white picket fences, quaint houses, and picturesque lawns. Sprinklers shoot jets of crystal-clear water high into the air and a gentle breeze rustles the trees.

The spell is suddenly broken as we hear the sound of HEAVY FOOTSTEPS slapping against the pavement.

ANDERSON CAVANAUGH, a handsome twenty-something, storms up to us, his dark hair plastered against his sweating forehead, and an OVER-THE-SHOULDER BOOKBAG bouncing against his hip.

Anderson glances to his left, toward the sidewalk, where THREE GENTLEMEN IN DARK SUITS stroll along, each one holding a STACK OF PAMPHLETS.

Anderson puts on the afterburner and bolts ahead of them, charging toward the end of the street. He turns in to the front lawn of the last house, a quaint colonial, and knocks on the door.

As he waits for an answer, we hear another set of footsteps behind us, and another YOUNG MAN enters frame, dressed to match Anderson in a short-sleeved dress shirt and striped tie.

He sports an identical shoulder bag.

Welcome ENZO VEGA (22), who stops just shy of us, his hands in his pockets as he looks down the street at Anderson, who is still waiting at the door.

Enzo faces front, his gaze directed our way.

> ENZO
> (to us)
> Right. So I'd be lying if I said I knew *exactly* what
> was going on...? But apparently, Anderson got

himself into this weird sort of financial clusterfuck that he's got like—four days to sell his way out of.

He quickly looks over his shoulder, just as the front door of the house swings open and Anderson steps through.

> ENZO (cont'd)
> (back to us)
> Honestly, I have no idea what the hell he's talking about—the guy's not really big on details... and the truth is, he could also be a little unbalanced, so... I dunno. I said I'd help him.
> (beat)
> Though I'm not exactly sure what that means now—

A sudden RUCKUS erupts at the end of the street and Enzo whirls around.

Anderson comes flying out of the colonial, tumbling down the steps so wildly that the contents of his bookbag go shooting out across the lawn. He hobbles back to his feet and starts charging our way, one of his hands wrapped in his necktie.

> ANDERSON
> Run!

> ENZO
> What?

> ANDERSON
> RUN!

Enzo shoots a wide-eyed glance at us, then peels off.

Anderson's near-empty bookbag slaps viciously against his hip, and as he approaches us, we see BLOOD smearing the front of his dress shirt and trickling down the hand bundled in his tie.

> ENZO (O.C.)
> (distant)
> Why are we running?!

Anderson pants uncontrollably and stumbles into a mailbox, where he disentangles his hand to assess the damage:
His MIDDLE FINGER is gone.

ANDERSON
(panting)
So much blood... so much fucking bl—

He passes out in a heap, and his SEVERED FINGER rolls out of his hand and into the road.

CUT TO BLACK.

Then TITLE OVER:
AMERICAN SALESMAN

CUT TO:

INT. CHURCH [SOLOMON CORPORATION REGIONAL OFFICE] – DAY

SUPER:
Solomon Corporation Regional Office
One Month Earlier

Anderson walks through a corridor, his eyes fixed on something written over the palm of his (fully-fingered) hand. He mutters to himself before glancing up at the numbers of the doors passing on either side of him.

He looks over his shoulder, glaring directly at us for awhile before setting off around the corner.

He passes the CHURCH OFFICES and several other rooms, then takes a series of turns, which leads him right past the church offices again.

Anderson stops to glance at his hand. He steals another look at us, then quickly sets off the other way.

He arrives at a door with a small slit of a window and stops to check the room number against the information on his hand.

Once verified, Anderson starts straightening his tie, but suddenly he pauses and looks down the corridor.

He sees us—and his face sets into a scowl.

SUPER:
Anderson Cavanaugh
New Recruit

INT. SUNDAY SCHOOL ROOM – CONTINUOUS

Anderson enters, shutting the door soundly behind him.

> ANDERSON
> Sorry I'm late. Some jackass was filming out there—

He turns to the room; his face falls as he glimpses us again.

The distinct, played-in appearance of the room is nicely offset by the group of ADULT BODIES packed in on the Fisher Price benches and plastic mini-chairs.

A twenty-ish BLONDE in a Hillary Clinton pantsuit strides out of the group and flicks a sheet of paper out of a briefcase.

> LILAH
> You need to sign this.

She takes a SILVER PEN out of her pocket and clicks the end before handing it off to Anderson.

> ANDERSON
> What is it?

> LILAH
> A release—which will give the corporation permission to use your image as part of our multimedia.

SUPER:

> Lilah Fairchild
> Solomon Corp. Organizational Leader

Anderson eyes the pen.

> ANDERSON
> Did… everyone…?

He looks around, and on second glance, he notices that the room is indeed full of people holding releases.

> VOICE (O.C.)
> And what if we don't sign?

Reveal UNKNOWN, who is also holding a release, but his face is BLURRED OUT.

> LILAH
> Then they'll blur you out and withhold your name.

                    UNKNOWN
                (crumpling his release)
            Good. 'Cause that's what I want.

Unfazed, Lilah puts the release on top of a book and shoves it toward Anderson,
who begins to sign.

                     LILAH
            We've traditionally skipped this unpleasantness—back
            when we used to contract out to Harrelson—but, as
            of September, Harrelson and the corporation have
            gone separate ways...

                    ANDERSON
                  (still signing)
            Oh, really? What was it, "creative diff"—?
                     LILAH
            He was euthanized.

Anderson freezes; the room is dead quiet.

                 LILAH (CONT'D)
            Tragic, I know, but—we're counting our blessings.
                   (whispering)
            He wasn't very good.

Lilah snatches the half-signed release away with a smile.

                 LILAH (CONT'D)
            Thank you.

INT. CORRIDOR – LATER

Lilah closes the door of the Sunday school room behind her. She takes a sheet
of card stock out of her briefcase and tapes the sign next to the entrance. It
reads, "RECRUIT HOLDING AREA."

She steps back, then decides to straighten the corners of the sign a few
millimeters.

Slowly she pries herself away and struts off.

EXT. CHURCH PARKING LOT – MEANWHILE

A FORD TAURUS peels in and double-parks across two handicap spots.

CLIFF HOLLOWAY—29, but strangely boyish—steps out in dark aviator glasses. He pulls a bookbag from the back seat of his car and locks the doors via remote control. He gives the ass-end of the Taurus a heavy slap and points to the model name.

> CLIFF
> (to us)
> You get a shot of that?

He suddenly steps up to camera, unnaturally close.

> CLIFF (CONT'D)
> (whispering)
> I call her Clit.
> (beat)
> Get it? Clit. Taurus...?

An uneasy beat passes.

SUPER:
> Cliff Holloway
> Field Manager

Cliff breaks the tension with a smirk.

> CLIFF (CONT'D)
> Hey, you wanna see something badass?

He takes the silence for a "yes," and his face pulls into an even wider smile.

> CLIFF (CONT'D)
> Okay. Check this out. Hold this a sec.

He hands his bookbag to an unseen crew person, then gestures us closer as he unlocks the trunk.

> CLIFF (CONT'D)
> Ready?

He pauses for dramatic effect; and then with a grin, Cliff throws the trunk open: the interior is layered with a stash of PORNOGRAPHIC MEDIA.

Cliff's smirk is unbearable. He throws his arm up and leans against the trunk in a would-be cool, James Dean sort of way.

> CLIFF (CONT'D)
> Private collection. I brought it 'cause I thought the boys could—

He makes a beating-off motion with his hand.

> CLIFF (CONT'D)
> You know—before we start enforcing abstinence.

> CLIFF (CONT'D)
> (beat)
> I'm pretty merciful that way.

He pulls a JUICE BOX from the pocket of his bomber jacket and pokes a straw through the top. He starts sipping grape juice through the corner of his mouth.

> CLIFF (CONT'D)
> Generally speaking, we have very strict rules against this sort of thing—

He gestures vaguely to the pornographic stash.

> CLIFF (CONT'D)
> But—what Corporate doesn't know doesn't hurt 'em, right?

He winks and takes to sipping his juice box again. It takes a moment, but the reality of the situation finally sinks in and Cliff looks directly at us, unflinchingly serious:

> CLIFF (CONT'D)
> You can edit all of this out, right?

INT. SUNDAY SCHOOL ROOM – LATER

Anderson's leg jitters beneath the pages of the BROCHURE in his hands: we see the typical, all-too-unreal images of smiling people enjoying corporate success. Emblazoned near the top:

THE SOLOMON DREAM
Opportunity... At Every Door

Several passages have been circled, but in this brief angle we can't make them out.

The BRUNETTE in the next chair shoots sidelong glances at him from the pages of GOOD CHRISTIAN LIVING. Anderson senses her eyes, folds up the brochure, and tucks it into his pocket. He loosens his tie a bit. There's a BLACK SMUDGE near the edge of his collar.

ANDERSON
(to the brunette)
Do you know…? Are we…?

He vaguely indicates the door, but the brunette shrugs and reseats herself so they won't have to meet eyes again.

Anderson strides to the door and shoves the crucifix-print drapes aside. He peers both ways down the corridor through the thin slit of a window, then turns back to the room.

He crosses to a window at the far end, throws it open and takes a seat on the sill.

He fiddles in his pockets for a while, then pulls out a cigarette. Anderson starts lighting up.

UNKNOWN
(beat)
Um, excuse me, but… you can't smoke in here.

ANDERSON
Shouldn't. "Can't" makes it seem impossible.

He clicks the lid of his Zippo shut and tucks the lighter away. Unknown rolls up his magazine and moves to the other side of the room. He's quickly replaced by—

ENZO
You got an extra?

Anderson turns and sizes up the newcomer.

SUPER:
Lorenzo Vega
New Recruit

An uncertain moment passes between them, and Anderson continues studying the guy's face.

ANDERSON
You smoke?

ENZO
No, I'm just… shopping for "normal."

Anderson smirks and hands him a Marlboro. Enzo sets the cigarette in his mouth and scans the room, almost as if seeing it for the first time.

> ENZO (CONT'D)
> Probably gonna be a lot less of it around here.

Anderson lights him up, watching carefully as Enzo takes the first drag. He's a natural.

> ANDERSON
> So you do smoke.

> ENZO
> Did.

He holds up the cigarette.

> ENZO (CONT'D)
> Here's to last times.

Anderson smiles, though not really at him. He glances out the window and lets the conversation die, until—

> ENZO (CONT'D)
> (beat)
> Enzo Vega.

Anderson catches the hand on his periphery and reanimates.

> ANDERSON
> (shaking)
> Anderson.

> ENZO
> So. What's your story, Anderson?
> (beat, off his look)
> Why are you here?

Anderson lets the question sink in, then smiles again.

> ENZO (CONT'D)
> Oh, you're one of those guys.
> (then)
> Noble sort. Here to bring religion and other such nonsense to we happy infidels.

                    ANDERSON
                 (re: the cigarette)
          Well this wouldn't be doing much for the image of
          my cause.

Enzo smirks.

                 ANDERSON (CONT'D)
          Your turn...
                 (he reads Enzo's NAMETAG)
          "Quixote."

A beat; Enzo shifts his weight, suddenly insecure.

                      ENZO
          Well, you know — I've got this sister, and... she kinda
          needs this eye surgery...? So... I came out here hoping
          to scrounge up enough cash to fix her up.

                    ANDERSON
          Are you serious?

                      ENZO
          No. That's just what I've been telling people since
          recruitment.
                 (beat)
          I think it adds character.

Anderson grins and turns back to the window.

Several quiet moments pass before the door swings open. Cliff enters with a stack
of SHRINK-WRAPPED CLOTHES underarm. The room settles into an odd
hush, save for the suction-y sound of Cliff sipping the last bit of liquid from his
juice box.
Anderson and Enzo put out their cigarettes.

                      CLIFF
          All right. I'm gonna need all the ladies to excuse
          themselves to the next room: we gentlemen have gotta
          get undressed. Unless you'd... rather stay and get a
          sampling of our merchandise.

The ladies collect themselves and sweep out, shooting disgusted looks at Cliff
on their way past.

Cliff smirks and shuts the door behind them.

                    CLIFF (CONT'D)
          Okay, fellas, these are your standard issue bookman's
          uniforms.

He starts flinging packages off his stack.

                    CLIFF (CONT'D)
          Your BMUs. Put 'em on and head out.

INT. CHURCH SANCTUARY - LATER

The recruits sit in the pews closest to the pulpit, whispering amongst themselves.
They are uniformly costumed in short-sleeved dress shirts and striped ties.

SUPER:
                    "Leviticus Company"
                 First Organizational Meeting

The back doors fly open and Lilah comes strutting down the aisle, drawing
stares as she passes.

She marches to the front of the sanctuary and pulls down a PROJECTION
SCREEN. She turns on her heel.

                    LILAH
          Welcome to basic training, L Company. You will
          here learn the skills necessary to survive and succeed
          on the bookfield. Now: many years of proper Christian
          education will teach you that there are four Gospels.
                    (beat)
          This is wrong.

She produces a thick book called "THE SOLOMON GUIDE."

                    LILAH (CONT'D)
          The Gospel According to Solomon. So called, because
          you will take everything within these pages as gospel
          truth. So—

She rattles the guide at them.

                    LILAH (CONT'D)
          Be doers of the word, and not hearers only.
She sets the book on the pulpit and smiles.

                    LILAH (CONT'D)
          All right, then. Let's begin.

She raises a remote control and clicks it at a projector.

The lights dim, and an image of a BOOKBAG begins to flicker onto the screen. As it solidifies, Lilah whips out a baton and smacks the point against the screen.

> LILAH (CONT'D)
> This is a standard issue Solomon Corporation Sampler Case. Also known as—

EXT. TRAINING AND EDUCATION PARK - DAY

> CLIFF
> A bookbag. Within it you will hold all necessary and appropriate product samples. It will never leave your sight.

He stands in front of the recruits with a bookbag raised overhead. He rotates a bit to make sure everyone gets a good look.

> CLIFF (CONT'D)
> Now repeat after me: "This is my bookbag."

LATER, the recruits stand in two parallel lines, cradling bookbags to their chests.

> RECRUITS
> This is my bookbag.

INTERCUT SANCTUARY / TRAINING AND EDUCATION PARK

Lilah paces the stretch of floor between the pulpit and the projector screen. The words "THE BOOKMAN'S CREED" are printed over her latest slide.

> LILAH
> There are many like it, but this one is mine.

IN THE PARK, we find the recruits and Cliff as before.

> RECRUITS
> There are many like it, but this one is mine.

Cliff steps up to Anderson, his face now just inches away.

> CLIFF
> My bookbag, without me, is useless.

> RECRUITS
> My bookbag, without me, is useless.

> CLIFF
> Without my bookbag... I am useless.

Anderson's knuckles whiten around his bookbag. Across from him, an overweight girl, HEATHER DAVIES, is fighting back tears.

> RECRUITS
> Without my bookbag, I am useless.

BACK IN THE SANCTUARY, Lilah stops pacing directly in the light of the projector and glares at her company.

> LILAH
> Before God, I swear this creed:

AT THE PARK, Cliff prowls alongside the lines of recruits, who continue to stand at rigid attention.

> RECRUITS
> My bookbag and myself are crusaders for His kingdom. We are masters of our enemy. So be it, until victory is His and we have made disciples of all nations.

INT. CHURCH SANCTUARY - RESUMING

Lilah smirks in the silence. The letters of her slide form eerie and sinister patterns over her face.

> LILAH
> (softly)
> Amen.

SMASH CUT TO:

INT. FELLOWSHIP HALL - LATER

Anderson takes a swig of GREEN PUNCH. He pulls the cup away and examines its contents.

> ANDERSON
> (to us)
> So, uh... they were having this Kool-Aid in the lobby.

He looks at the cup from another angle.

> ANDERSON (CONT'D)
> (beat)
> I've never seen this color before...

EXT. TRAINING AND EDUCATIONAL PARK - AFTERNOON

The recruits are double-timing in formation. They all have bookbags slung over their shoulders.

Cliff runs on the side of the block, leading the recruits through a rousing refrain of "What a Friend We Have in Jesus."

Lilah stands a ways off, poised for interview as the company passes in the background.

> LILAH
> People are always talking about indoctrination. We do not "indoctrinate" here.

> CLIFF
> SING, GODDAMNIT! SING LOUDER!

The marching song swells, and despite the interruption, Lilah stares adamantly forward.

> LILAH
> Yes, I'll admit, there's a strong push for conformity, but... if we're divided, then... what hope is there for the heathen peoples of the world?

INT. TRAINING AND EDUCATION PARK - LATER

The company comes to a stop. Several people are throwing up; Lilah and Cliff step casually around the vomit, handing PILLS to the recruits.

> LILAH
> This is a multivitamin supplement.

She raises a CAPSULE into the air.

> LILAH (CONT'D)
> A typical bookfield diet is, unfortunately, lacking in certain essential vitamins and nutrients. In order for the body of the salesman to stay in top form, the Solomon Corporation has provided you these pills.

                    CLIFF
        The sensation that some of you are feeling is not just
        because you are a bunch of fat-bodies. If you do not
        take these pills and maintain a Guide-approved diet,
        you will puke your fucking guts out.

Without thinking, Lilah holds out a large jar. A huge label on the side reads:
SWEAR JAR. Cliff drops a quarter in.

                    LILAH
                (to the recruits)
        And let me be clear: these are one-a-day pills. You
        need to take one now with your Kool-Aid.

ANGLE ON Anderson, who's standing a couple of yards away from the group,
ready for interview.

                    ANDERSON
                    (to us)
        When I was twelve, my parents enrolled me in this
        weird-ass vacation Bible school. The reason I bring it
        up is because—from a specific point of view—this is
        kinda the same thing.
                    (beat)
        Only on crack.

He lifts up his KING JAMES FEATHERWEIGHT SAMPLER.

                    ANDERSON (CONT'D)
        We go door to door—selling *this*. Gotta be pretty
        desperate, huh?

He smirks, but he's not really amused. Suddenly—

                    LILAH (O.C.)
        Cavanaugh.

                    ANDERSON
        Yeah?

Anderson tucks his sampler away as Lilah walks up. She shoves a multivitamin
and a cup of Kool-Aid into his hands.

                    LILAH
        Take your pill.

Anderson swigs the capsule down.

CHILDREN'S/YOUNG ADULT FICTION WINNERS

1 **Tom Clark**
Loveland OH

2 **Sarah Tregay**
Eagle ID

3 **Tamara R White**
Williamsburg VA

4 **Lori Straub**
Mount Pleasant SC

5 **Patti J. Kurtz**
Minot ND

6 **Susan Harrison**
Great Falls MT

7 **Stacy McAnulty**
Kernersville NC

8 **Bev Goodman**
Scarborough ON Canada

9 **Sharon Dexter**
Lake Geneva WI

10 **Jessica Saigh**
Saint Louis MO

11 **Bonnie Terry**
Sheridan AR

12 **Donna M. McDine**
Tappan NY

13 **Kathleen Cherry**
Kitimat BC Canada

14 **Brian Rock**
Chesterfield VA

15 **Samuel Ferguson**
Orem UT

16 **Wendi Richards**
Fairfield ME

17 **Nancy Ellen Hird**
Hayward CA

18 **Sandy Steers**
Fawnskin CA

19 **Kathleen Cherry**
Kitimat BC Canada

20 **Ben Baskin**
Cleveland OH

21 **Jean Reagan**
Salt Lake City UT

22 **Judy Irvin Kuns**
Sandusky OH

23 **Lois Avrick**
Delray Beach FL

24 **Christina Struyk-Bonn**
Portland OR

25 **Chelena Blount**
Charlotte NC

26 **Dawn Malone**
Chenoa IL

27 **Martha Cobb Heneisen**
Rome GA

28 **Ariel Hoffman**
Novi MI

29 **Alan Druckman**
Seaford NY

30 **Laurie Alloway**
San Diego CA

31 **Laura Ayo**
Knoxville TN

32 **Patricia Jackson**
Centennial CO

33 **Gregory Stephen Fields**
Fort Lauderdale FL

34 **Gregory Stephen Fields**
Fort Lauderdale FL

35 **Elizabeth A. Roberts**
Denver CO

36 **Gail L. Vannelli**
Thousand Oaks CA

37 **Karen Schulz**
Stillwater MN

38 **Tom Salyers**
Greenfield OH

39 **Kimberly Dana**
Culver City CA

40 **Debra Sayble-Thornbrugh**
Oceanside CA

41 **Janet Schultz**
Saint Peter MN

42 **Colleen M. Story**
Idaho Falls ID

43 **Karen Beaumont**
Capitola CA

44 **Nancy Carney**
Pueblo CO

45 **Kathryn Cryan**
Glastonbury CT

46 **Jessica Schaub**
Lansing MI

47 **Kathryn Cryan**
Glastonbury CT

48 **Jessica Schaub**
Lansing MI

49 **Suzanne Morrone**
San Jose CA

50 **Laurie Alloway**
San Diego CA

51 **Michael Hager**
Ventura CA

52 **M. J. Smith**
Scottsdale AZ

53 **Tracy A. Gentry**
Fairview MO

54 **Judy Crowder**
Morehead City NC

55 **Jeff Kirkendall**
Chino Valley AZ

56 **Kimberly Dana**
Culver City CA

57 **Tim O'Hara**
Elk Grove CA

58 **Jaclyn Jaeger**
Danvers MA

59 **Christina Steiner**
Simi Valley CA

60 **Chelena Blount**
Charlotte NC

61 **Bart Oxley**
Belmont CA

62 **Lou DiGiuseppe**
Syracuse NY

63 **Dorothy Forman, OSF/T**
Tiffin OH

64 **Francesca Sagala**
New Buffalo MI

65 **Jonas Roberts**
Hartford CT

66 **Erin E. Calicic**
Murrysville PA

67 **Jean Reagan**
Salt Lake City UT

68 **Patricia R. Cardarelli**
Lorain OH

69 **Bobbi Porter**
Anchorage AK

70 **Tatiana Los Reed**
Trenton NJ

71 **Lisa Carpenter**
Colorado Springs CO

72 **Eugene Orlando**
Seffner FL

73 **Sheri Dillard**
Atlanta GA

74 **Roshaunda D. Cade**
University City MO

75 **Kim Lippert**
Paicines CA

76 **Gail L. Vannelli**
Thousand Oaks CA

77 **Syrl Ann Kazlo**
Fort Ann NY

78 **Denise L. Ungerman**
Feasterville PA

79 **Eugene Orlando**
Seffner FL

80 **Richelle Pipho-Holle**
Oskaloosa IA

81 **Linda M. Pickett**
Kalamazoo MI

82 **Nancy Shelton**
Springfield MO

83 **Daniel Fonder**
North Brunswick NJ

84 **Lori Anastasia**
North Attleboro MA

85 **Carla Richardson**
Roanoke Rapids NC

86 **Janice Levy**
Merrick NY

87 **S. A. Harris**
Eureka MO

88 **Deborah Melnik**
Athens GA

89 **Rose Nelson**
Greenville NC

90 **Donna Yarbrough Gandy**
Tyler TX

91 **Donna Yarbrough Gandy**
Tyler TX

92 **Virginia Wilson**
Trout Lake MI

93 **Jessica Saigh**
Saint Louis MO

94 **John M. Scanlan**
Hilton Head Island SC

95 **Allyson Denise Walker**
Fairfax VA

96 **Allyson Denise Walker**
Fairfax VA

97 **M. P. Liebchen**
Altavista VA

98 **Katie Brown**
San Gabriel CA

99 **Keith R. Smith**
Brawley CA

100 **Fred Philipson**
Gilbert AZ

FEATURE ARTICLE WINNERS

1 **April Love Bailey**
   Chicago IL
2 **Vicki Huffman**
   Mt. Juliet TN
3 **Stephen Densmore**
   Poughkeepsie NY
4 **Mary Keating**
   Pocatello ID
5 **Karen Kassel Hutto**
   Dacula GA
6 **Mary Keating**
   Pocatello ID
7 **Charles Capaldi**
   Derby VT
8 **Christopher Lyden**
   Kalaheo HI
9 **Ann Weaver**
   Saint Petersburg FL
10 **Riley N. Kelly**
   Excel AL
11 **Karen Kassel Hutto**
   Dacula GA
12 **Joannie A. Netzler**
   Modesto CA
13 **Ruth Welburn**
   Sidney BC Canada
14 **Corinne Friesen**
   Surrey BC Canada
15 **Brian Trent**
   Waterbury CT
16 **Nic Brown**
   Lexington KY
17 **Ann Weaver**
   Saint Petersburg FL
18 **Carole Firstman**
   Visalia CA
19 **Joe Luca**
   Glendale CA
20 **Ann Weaver**
   Saint Petersburg FL
21 **Richard Thayer**
   Thomasville NC
22 **James D. Shelby**
   Oroville CA
23 **Kelly J. Stigliano**
   Orange Park FL
24 **Blaire Briody**
   New York NY
25 **Kristy Arbon**
   St. Louis MO
26 **Donald Vaughan**
   Raleigh NC
27 **Carrie Lynn Goddard**
   Los Angeles CA
28 **Robert A. Lindblom**
29 **Olga Bonfiglio**
   Kalamazoo MI
30 **Patricia Herchuk Sheehy**
   Wethersfield CT
31 **Caroline Ahlswede**
   Newark CA
32 **Connie Bickman**
   Cannon Falls MN
33 **Sandra Chambers**
   Leland NC
34 **Donald Vaughan**
   Raleigh NC

35 **Carole Firstman**
   Visalia CA
36 **Carole Firstman**
   Visalia CA
37 **Laura Bloch Bourque**
   Peterborough NH
38 **Kay Grant**
   Albuquerque NM
39 **Amy Carrasco**
   Layton UT
40 **Michele Herman**
   New York NY
41 **Melissa Crytzer Fry**
   Mammoth AZ
42 **Chris Hare**
   Moorpark CA
43 **Teresa H. Berger, MBA**
   Abington PA
44 **Leonard Morse**
   Silver Spring MD
45 **Kirsten Bell, PhD**
   Vancouver BC Canada
46 **Bob Canning**
   Petaluma CA
47 **Karen H. Phillips**
   Flintstone GA
48 **Sandra Chambers**
   Leland NC
49 **Yolanda (Linda) Reid Chassiakos**
   Long Beach CA
50 **Donald Vaughan**
   Raleigh NC
51 **Claire Yezbak Fadden**
   Chula Vista CA
52 **Lois J. Funk**
   Manito IL
53 **Frank Kosa**
   Santa Monica CA
54 **Mary Keating**
   Pocatello ID
55 **Donna Reames Rich**
   Pine Mountain GA
56 **Sandra Rossetti Mitchell**
   Peoria IL
57 **Jason Miller**
   Kittanning PA
58 **Henry I. Kurtz**
   Bronx NY
59 **Heidi Krumenauer**
   Stoughton WI
60 **Jim Pettengill**
   Ridgway CO
61 **Tracy Burton**
   Midland MI
62 **Kirsten Bell, PhD**
   Vancouver BC Canada
63 **James Church**
   Easton MD
64 **Scott M. Fisher**
   Allerton IA
65 **Casey L. Penn**
   Benton AR
66 **Mary Lee Blackwell**
   Old Saybrook CT
67 **Art Busse**
   Berkeley CA
68 **Patrick P. Astre, CFP, EA, RFC**
   Ridge NY

69 **George Heiring**
   Eatonton GA
70 **Barbara Lloyd Nelson**
   Wauseon OH
71 **Melissa Siig**
   Tahoe City CA
72 **A. M. Mooquin**
   Aurora ON Canada
73 **Suzanne Morrone**
   San Jose CA
74 **Shaun Manning**
   New York NY
75 **Jason Krump**
   Pullman WA
76 **Robert A. Lindblom**
77 **Donal Blaise Lloyd**
   Germantown NY
78 **Art Busse**
   Berkeley CA
79 **Chanan Tigay**
   San Francisco CA
80 **Jason Krump**
   Pullman WA
81 **Claire Yezbak Fadden**
   Chula Vista CA
82 **Pamela Dittmer McKuen**
   Glen Ellyn IL
83 **Kay Grant**
   Albuquerque NM
84 **Anne Lawrence Guyon**
   Saxtons River VT
85 **Pamela Gibson**
   Mililani HI
86 **Christy Heitger**
   Bloomington IN
87 **T. Joan Pleines**
   Lake Wales FL
88 **Olga Bonfiglio**
   Kalamazoo MI
89 **Kathy Gilk**
   Melrose MN
90 **Cecily Hamlin Wells**
   Hendersonville NC
91 **Wayne and Treba Thompson**
   Birmingham AL
92 **Jim Pettengill**
   Ridgway CO
93 **James D. Shelby**
   Oroville CA
94 **Naomi Freeman**
   Toronto ON Canada
95 **Susy Flory**
   Castro Valley CA
96 **Patricia Herchuk Sheehy**
   Wethersfield CT
97 **Scott Patrick Wagner**
   Oxnard CA
98 **La Ronda Bowen**
   Pasadena CA
99 **Anne Lawrence Guyon**
   Saxtons River VT
100 **Martha R. Kane**
   Canton CT

GENRE SHORT STORY WINNERS

1 R.K. Chandler
Monterey CA

2 Melanie L. McCree
Vancouver WA

3 David M. Thomas
Monterey CA

4 Kathryn Cryan
Glastonbury CT

5 Lisa Cobb Sabatini
Exeter PA

6 Patricia Little
Beaverton OR

7 Bennett R. Hipps
Midland GA

8 Matthew Maybray

9 Gerry Griffiths
San Jose CA

10 Christin Haws
Clinton IL

11 Roberta M. Pala
Centreville VA

12 Kimberly Yerina
Marilla NY

13 Tracy Tandy
San Rafael CA

14 Nikki Deckon
Wilsonville OR

15 James David Robertson
Uijeongbu-si South Korea

16 Victoria Ohlin
Akron OH

17 Eric Westley
Arlington VA

18 James Howard
Buffalo NY

19 Bennett R. Hipps
Midland GA

20 Twyla Martin
Grand Junction CO

21 David Buffum
Brooklyn NY

22 Stephanie Burkhart
Castaic CA

23 Charles Warren
Bartow FL

24 Nicholas V. HeartMan
Mason OH

25 Gerry Griffiths
San Jose CA

26 Ken R. Zibell
Milwaukee WI

27 Richard D. Smith
Tyrone GA

28 Gary L. Caldwell
Gainesville TX

29 Marcia Womack
Chicago IL

30 Elaine Kolumba
Victoria Ohlin
Aurora OH

31 Teresa Little
Jacksonville FL

32 Dee Alessandra Sugalski
Charleston TN

33 Chris Boyle
Hendersonville TN

34 Summer Dalgarn
Meridian ID

35 Jim Grigsby
Sebastian FL

36 Irv Haberman
Richmond Hill ON Canada

37 Donovan R. Walling
Bloomington IN

38 Linda Aschbrenner
Marshfield WI

39 Donovan R. Walling
Bloomington IN

40 L. Guy LeVee
Eldersburg MD

41 Natalie Wasmer
Dallas TX

42 Lew Osteen
Sacramento CA

43 Stephen M. Clark
Louisville KY

44 Michael Lawson
Cincinnati OH

45 Michele Kramer
South Amboy NJ

46 Christopher Ryan
New Milford NJ

47 Shelby Beckett
Tulsa OK

48 L. B. Garman
Longmont CO

49 Andrew Peterson
Bradley CA

50 Mark W. Moronell, M.D.
Anchorage AK

51 Mark D. Moronell, MD
Anchorage AK

52 Joanna John
Atlanta GA

53 Jill M. Gordon
Prairie Du Chien WI

54 Jennifer M. Leach
Washington DC

55 John Yarrow
Pretoria South Africa

56 Amanda Sinquefield
Olive Branch MS

57 Louise Furley McRorie
Fort Lauderdale FL

58 Pierre-Alexandre Sicart
Xindian City Taipei County Taiwan,
Republic of China

59 Deborah Nold
Yuba City CA

60 Dan Balman
Marcellus NY

61 Christopher Kokoski
Jeffersonville IN

62 Laurel Wilczek
Saylorsburg PA

63 Gene Andrew Hoback
Lake Elsinore CA

64 Jim Phillips
Saginaw MN

65 Debbie Gillette
Fort Worth TX

66 John Hirtle
Greenland NH

67 Gerry Griffiths
San Jose CA

68 Elyse Moran
Marshfield MA

69 Susan K. Salzer
Columbia MO

70 Robert A. Lindblom

71 Charlotte Cohen
Westminster CA

72 Richard M. Bauer
Langley WA

73 Stephen Cvengros
Redmond WA

74 Billie Travalini
Wilmington DE

75 Herbert Spohn
Topeka KS

76 Trevor Titus
Owatonna MN

77 Kelly Murray
Mount Horeb WI

78 Morton M. Rumberg
Rancho Cordova CA

79 Billie Travalini
Wilmington DE

80 Patrick Klingaman
Kittery ME

81 Brian James
Columbia SC

82 Nikki Deckon
Wilsonville OR

83 Mark E. Daugherty
Staunton VA

84 Heather Patterson
Bloomington IL

85 Silke Chambers
Boardman OH

86 Marie Anderson
La Grange IL

87 J.R. Beau
La Grande OR

88 Jim Marion Etter
Bethany OK

89 Carla J. Trabert
Columbia City IN

90 Charlotte Ehney
Greenwood SC

91 Richard A. Standring
Pembroke MA

92 Teresa Freeman Cravens
Manchester TN

93 James F. Smith
St Augustine FL

94 Brianne Linn
Lock Haven PA

95 Jaimie Frattolillo
Hamilton Square NJ

96 P. B. Fox
Coarsegold CA

97 Sharon Wahl
Katy TX

98 Katie Harris Richardson
Havre MT

99 David M. Thomas
Monterey CA

100 Toni Salyers
Greenfield OH

INSPIRATIONAL WRITING WINNERS

1 **Diana K. Williams**
Crystal Springs FL

2 **Mal King**
Santa Paula CA

3 **Joann White**
Saranac Lake NY

4 **Donna Arlynn Frisinger**
Rochester IN

5 **Christopher Ryan**
New Milford NJ

6 **Tess Almendarez Lojacono**
East Aurora NY

7 **Tess Almendarez Lojacono**
East Aurora NY

8 **Louise R. Shaw**
North Salt Lake UT

9 **Katrina De Man**
Rockford MI

10 **Nancy Drummond**
Tigard OR

11 **Caroline Castle Hicks**
Huntersville NC

12 **Kelly O'Dell Stanley**
Crawfordsville IN

13 **Joann White**
Saranac Lake NY

14 **Nicole Kalstein**
Woodinville WA

15 **J. Griffith**

16 **Meezie Hermansen**

17 **Mid Stutsman**
Goshen IN

18 **Josh Jutler**
Cuyahoga Falls OH

19 **Sarah Schaffner**
Baltimore MD

20 **George Heiring**
Eatonton GA

21 **Kelly O'Dell Stanley**
Crawfordsville IN

22 **Nick Chamberlain**
Wiggins CO

23 **Russel Jarvis**
Wilkinson IN

24 **Deborah Flarity**
Spring TX

25 **Judith P. Nembhard**
Chattanooga TN

26 **Aimee Leon**
Los Angeles CA

27 **Kathleen Pooler**
Amsterdam NY

28 **James A. Schieldge**
Arcadia CA

29 **Elizabeth MacDonald Burrows**
Seattle WA

30 **Elizabeth MacDonald Burrows**
Seattle WA

31 **Barry Brakeville**
Kansas City MO

32 **Polly House**
Nashville TN

33 **Andrea**
Brownsville OR

34 **Johnese Burtram**
Warrenton VA

35 **Karin Fuller**
South Charleston WV

36 **Lina Zeldovich**
Woodside NY

37 **Christina Summers**
Hillbank Australia

38 **Cindy R. Williams**
Gilbert AZ

39 **Amy Wickland**
Hales Corners WI

40 **Sharon Kramer**
Wheaton IL

41 **Lisa Peters**
Georgetown MA

42 **Anna Dao**
New York NY

43 **Gerry L Cofield**
Wedowee AL

44 **Kathy Green**
Evanston IL

45 **Marcia A. Mitchell**
Port Orchard WA

46 **Walter Ratliff**
Herndon VA

47 **C. A. Rypel**
Cleveland OH

48 **Duane Culbertson**
Burlington MA

49 **Kim Fletcher Bowden**
Augusta GA

50 **Lisa Egle**
Millburn NJ

51 **Stephen Densmore**
Poughkeepsie NY

52 **Wm. Douglas Van Devender**
Beebe AR

53 **Eileen Rutt Graybill**
Leola PA

54 **Catherine Al-Meten**
Monterey CA

55 **Lana Danielle Jacobson**
Johannesburg South Africa

56 **Jacqueline Mendez (JAX)**
San Antonio TX

57 **Daryl Khaw**
Portland OR

58 **Alisan Peters**
Jackson WY

59 **Nick Chamberlain**
Wiggins CO

60 **Richard Martin**
Charlottesville VA

61 **Jan I. Berlage**
Monkton MD

62 **Brenda F. Ring**
Cullman AL

63 **Lisa Young**
West Keansburg NJ

64 **Louis M. Profeta, MD**
Indianapolis IN

65 **Richard Martin**
Charlottesville VA

66 **Sandy Fink**
Dowling Park FL

67 **FRANK S. CONTE**
Bronx NY

68 **Jackie Mills**
Brainerd MN

69 **September Vaudrey**
Inverness IL

70 **Cindy Lens**
Amherst NH

71 **Julie Harrison**
West Baden Springs IN

72 **Pamala J. Vincent**
Eagle Creek OR

73 **Vicky M. Semones**
Oakland CA

74 **Sheryl Boldt**
Tallahassee FL

75 **Barbara Pritchard**
Las Vegas NV

76 **Cherilyn DeAguero**
San Clemente CA

77 **J. Graham Ducker**
Oshawa ON Canada

78 **Holly Coop**
Joliet IL

79 **Ronald T. Brown**
Chandler AZ

80 **Martha Cobb Heneisen**
Rome GA

81 **Shaileen Volpe**
Millis MA

82 **Marcia Alexander**
Chula Vista CA

83 **Bunmi Ishola**
Evanston IL

84 **Martha R. Fehl**
Brookville IN

85 **Pamela Malo**
Guilderland NY

86 **Solange Arbesu-Sala**
San Francisco CA

87 **Mary Jo Guglielmo**
Chicago IL

88 **Janet Grogan Olson**
Germantown TN

89 **Diane Hobaugh**
Santa Rosa CA

90 **Bunmi Ishola**
Evanston IL

91 **Lisa Williamson**
Birmingham AL

92 **Eileen Bassett**
Dawson Creek BC Canada

93 **Lou Conquest**
Colorado Springs CO

94 **Kim Fletcher Bowden**
Augusta GA

95 **Meadow Rue Merrill**
Bath ME

96 **Rebecca Luttrell Briley**
Pahoa HI

97 **Klara Dannar**
Dexter MI

98 **Becky Tidberg**
Neillsville WI

99 **Julie Anne Gardner**
Slidell LA

100 **Judy Crowder**
Morehead City NC

MAINSTREAM/LITERARY SHORT STORY WINNERS

1 **David F. Hamilton**
Santa Clarita CA

2 **Linda Aschbrenner**
Marshfield WI

3 **David Bate**
s Hollywood FL

4 **Gail Burwell**
Ypsilanti MI

5 **Nancy E. Trudel**
Morgantown WV

6 **Kelsea Best**
Brentwood TN

7 **Bill Carrigan**
Sarasota FL

8 **Stephanie Burkhart**
Castaic CA

9 **Max Newton**
Berkeley CA

10 **K.P. Robbins**
Harpers Ferry WV

11 **Marcia Corbino**
Sarasota FL

12 **Alisa D. May**
Spokane WA

13 **Rita M. Rohr**
Columbus OH

14 **Patrick Heggy**
Lakewood CO

15 **Natalie Telis**
Campbell CA

16 **Tracy Daniels**
Colonial Heights VA

17 **Jill V. Svoboda**
Nobleton FL

18 **Catherine Bronson**
St. Petersburg FL

19 **Paige Walton**
Canyon Lake TX

20 **Karon Sue Semones**
Roanoke VA

21 **Lisa Romano Licht**
Congers NY

22 **Josh Staub**
Hanover PA

23 **Joel Macht**
Hilton Head Island SC

24 **Ramona Scarborough**
Salem OR

25 **Kathleen Tomko**
Brookings OR

26 **Susan Tanenbaum**
New York NY

27 **David Maring**
Georgetown SC

28 **James K. Best**
Rochester MN

29 **Cherie Von Rosen**
Centennial CO

30 **John M. Scanlan**
Hilton Head Island SC

31 **Twyla Ellis**
Crosby TX

32 **Richard N. Valentine**
Palm Harbor FL

33 **Pierre-Alexandre Sicart**
Xindian City Taipei Taiwan,
Republic of China

34 **Shane Marquardt**
Nashville TN

35 **Rita Ciresi**
Wesley Chapel FL

36 **Helen E. Seebold**
Cary NC

37 **David F. Hamilton**
Santa Clarita CA

38 **David Molyneux**
Dansville NY

39 **Shane Marquardt**
Nashville TN

40 **Stephen Joseph**
Bangalore India

41 **Sharon Dwyer**
Sorrento FL

42 **Cora Kerr**
El Cajon

43 **Michael Willems**
Calgary AB Canada

44 **Taraz**
Gainesville FL

45 **Raya Saksouk**
Grosse Pointe MI

46 **Melanie Johnson**
Gainesville GA

47 **Joeby Dae Barham**
Reno NV

48 **Maureen Kay**
Vancouver WA

49 **Leslie A. Nelson**
Salisbury MD

50 **Bill Gregg**
Louisville KY

51 **Robin Archaumbault**
Bristol RI

52 **Susan Tannenbaum**
New York NY

53 **Patrick**
Williamsville NY

54 **Janet Kleinman**
Delray Beach FL

55 **Joyce A. Palmer**
Fort Myers FL

56 **Susan Tannenbaum**
New York NY

57 **Ms. Jerry Fisher**
Fresno CA

58 **Maxine Hart**
Gainesville FL

59 **Jean Cottrell Pence**
Ruskin FL

60 **Mary M. Hahn**
Richland Center WI

61 **Janice Spielberger**
San Antonio TX

62 **Bill Carrigan**
Sarasota FL

63 **Kathryn Hillis**
Melbourne FL

64 **Titjana Artop**
Saint Cloud FL

65 **Bill Carrigan**
Sarasota FL

66 **Charles J. Hiers**
Tempe AZ

67 **Randy Susan Meyers**
Boston MA

68 **Dorian Alu**
Belvidere NJ

69 **Scarlett Annadeus Baker**
Austin TX

70 **Sarah Weiler**
Kansas City MO

71 **Tricia Gropper**
Tucson AZ

72 **Leonard Tuchyner**
Barboursville VA

73 **Barbara Villemez**
Las Cruces NM

74 **Lynne Holzhausen (Eining)**
East Greenwich RI

75 **Laurie Kolp**
Beaumont TX

76 **Charles L. O'Connell**
Kitchener ON Canada

77 **Cheryl Spanos**
Lafayette CA

78 **Cheryl Spanos**
Lafayette CA

79 **Amina Gautier**
Saint Louis MO

80 **Daryl Miller**
Zurich Switzerland

81 **Maureen Clarke**
Goffstown NH

82 **David Bates**
Hollywood FL

83 **Pam Haringsma**
Hot Springs National Park AR

84 **Naomi Freeman**
Toronto ON Canada

85 **J. Steven Carr**
Mooresville NC

86 **Ellen M. Francisco**
Running Springs CA

87 **Lisa Taub**
Brooklyn NY

88 **Kevin Noschese**
Fairfield CT

89 **Naomi Freeman**
Toronto ON Canada

90 **Abir Wood**
Tulsa OK

91 **Carol Terry**
Newtown CT

92 **Martha Cobb Heneisen**
Rome GA

93 **J. Steven Carr**
Mooresville NC

94 **Craig Nybo**
Kaysville UT

95 **Michael Weddle**
Lonaconing MD

96 **Connie Mayo**
Chapmansboro TN

97 **Ruth Kibler Peck**
Dayton OH

98 **Erlinda Villamor Kravetz**
Leonardo NJ

99 **Danny Brantley**
Brandon MS

100 **Julia Oh**

MEMOIR/PERSONAL ESSAY WINNERS

1   Jamie Rotham
    Columbus OH
2   Sandra Staton-Taiwo
    York PA
3   Melissa Barnes
    Kirkland WA
4   Katherine Hengel
    Minneapolis MN
5   Beatrice Georgalidis
    Brooklyn NY
6   Holly Thomas
    Sullivan IL
7   Georgia Hoffman
    Sandy OR
8   Dawn Carter
    Richmond VA
9   Sarah Allen
    Provo UT
10 Lavon Hood
    Clarksdale MS
11 Brandy Snider
    Sandy UT
12 Laurie Balbo
    Little Falls NJ
13 Matthew DeFaveri
    Marietta GA
14 Christine W. Ross
    Glens Falls NY
15 Luigi A. Barney
    Latham NY
16 Henry C. Jadow
    New York NY
17 Elizabeth Black
    Douglas WY
18 Charity Whisman
    Middletown IN
19 Tim Johnson
    West Linn OR
20 Mary-Jane Gallienne
    Waterdown ON Canada
21 Tina Jin
    Toronto ON Canada
22 Damon Brown
    Newfield NJ
23 Patricia Jackson
    Englewood CO
24 Debra Sayble-Thornbrugh
    Oceanside CA
25 Katrice R. Cyphers
    Portland OR
26 Flora Reekstin
    Littleton CO
27 T. C. Tanis
    Englewood NJ
28 Tom Morris
    Lynchburg VA
29 Anita Jensen Mitchell
    Salt Lake City UT
30 R. Thomas Fox
    Laguna Beach CA
31 Laura Knight
    Orlando FL
32 Alice L. George
    Philadelphia PA
33 Thelma Adams
    Hyde Park NY
34 Gail Strickland
    Belvedere-Tiburon CA

35 Karl Williams
    Tunkhannock PA
36 Hilary Hansen
    Reisterstown MD
37 Elizabeth Emerson
    Kennebunk ME
38 Richard Thayer
    Thomasville NC
39 Sonja Stone
    Scottsdale AZ
40 G. Robert Zambs
    Fairhope AL
41 Josh Butler
    Cuyahoga Falls OH
42 Linda Moor Anelli
    West Dover VT
43 Joanne E. Dumene
    Alexandria VA
44 Simone Mimbs
    Oxnard CA
45 Rachael Hanel
    Madison Lake MN
46 September Vaudrey
    Inverness IL
47 Richard E. Reed
    Nashville TN
48 Jocelyn Krieger
    Boca Raton FL
49 Walter Rein
    Micaville NC
50 Meghan Krein
    Scottsdale AZ
51 Michele Herman
    New York NY
52 Paula Surrey
    Auburn ME
53 Dodie Cross
    Chelan WA
54 Vicki Nagel
    Van Nuys CA
55 Mary Kolesnikova
    San Francisco CA
56 Katherine Baker
    Philadelphia PA
57 Lana Danielle Jacobson
    Johannesburg South Africa
58 Joan Smith
    Seal Beach CA
59 Carrie Friedman
    Los Angeles CA
60 Daniel Fonder
    North Brunswick NJ
61 Linda Wentz
    Port Angeles WA
62 Donna Reames Rich
    Pine Mountain GA
63 Art Hoskins
    Libertyville IL
64 Arlene Scott
    Tarpon Springs FL
65 Linda Hudson Hoagland
    North Tazewell VA
66 Joseph Pantatello
    Levittown NY
67 Mary A. Best
    Rochester MN
68 Allan C. Stover
    The Villages FL

69 L. M. Smelser, Ph.D.
    Brighton MI
70 George Heiring
    Eatonton GA
71 Cheryl S. Smith
    Port Angeles WA
72 Pamela B. Blake
    Freeport ME
73 Kathy Connor
    Madison CT
74 J.T. Damiani
    Jacksonville FL
75 Jodie Platt
    California CA
76 Janice Edelman
    Huntingdon Valley PA
77 Rhonda Leverett
    The Woodlands TX
78 Monica James
    Merrick NY
79 Martha Culp
    Johnson City TN
80 David W. Page
    Wilmington VT
81 Susanne Lee
    Moorpark CA
82 Anna F. Hess
    Napa CA
83 Arnot McCallum
    Tecumseh ON Canada
84 Denise Amber Ryan
    Payson AZ
85 Lynda Zacharias
    Wellfleet MA
86 Elaine McFarland Radney
    Colorado Springs CO
87 Valerie Cole
    Rochester NY
88 Catherine Denton
    Tulsa OK
89 Fran Hooker
    Saint Louis MO
90 Denise Amber Ryan
    Payson AZ
91 Jacqueline Martin
    Westcliffe CO
92 Sandra Bellissimo
    Whitefish MT
93 Carol L. Scot
    Lansing MI
94 Aline Kuhl
    Cincinnati OH
95 Eleanor Oakes
    Phoenix AZ
96 Lynn Hartsell
    Paradise CA
97 Lora L. Crommett
    Lake San Marcos CA
98 Jill Pertler
    Cloquet MN
99 Elizabeth C. Hueben
    Sugar Land TX
100 M. K. Landstein
    Clermont FL

NON-RHYMING POETRY WINNERS

1. **Kathleen Olive Palmer**
   Fort Lauderdale FL
2. **Lee Netzler**
   Longmont CO
3. **Sybil L. Holloway**
   Bloomsburg PA
4. **Norma J. Lipp**
   Kalispell MT
5. **Susan Calderone**
   Brownsville PA
6. **Nicholas Yovanovick**
   Hastings MI
7. **Sachiko Ogawara**
   Rohnert Park CA
8. **Shirley Windward**
   Santa Monica CA
9. **William B. Young**
   Chapel Hill NC
10. **Chris Lord**
    Ann Arbor MI
11. **Gerald A. Winter**
    Manchester Twp NJ
12. **Ed Ridgley**
    Phenix City AL
13. **Dallas Huth**
    Santa Fe NM
14. **Clair Hsu Accomando**
    Bonita CA
15. **Monica Landy**
    Tenafly NJ
16. **Monica Landy**
    Tenafly NJ
17. **Mary Davis Brown**
    Lima OH
18. **Shakuntala Rajagopal**
    Algonquin IL
19. **Leah Schulte**
    Missoula MT
20. **Charles Sharpe**
    Seattle WA
21. **Kathleen Olive Palmer**
    Fort Lauderdale FL
22. **Nanette Dickson**
    Los Angeles CA
23. **R.F. Sedlack**
    Sarasota FL
24. **Christa R. Fordham**
    Parlin NJ
25. **Christa R. Fordham**
    Parlin NJ
26. **C. Victor Deloe**
    Richwood WV
27. **R.H. Peat**
    Auburn CA
28. **Maria Ercilla**
    Los Angeles CA
29. **Maria Ercilla**
    Los Angeles CA
30. **Jane P Morgan**
    Shippensburg PA
31. **Sheryl L. Nelms**
    Clyde TX
32. **Alex Gotowski**
    Mount Joy PA
33. **Sarah Lauderdale**
    Huntley IL
34. **John K. Rutenberg**
    Myrtle Beach SC

35. **Marge Steinert**
    Charles City IA
36. **Marie K. Wood**
    Sun City Center FL
37. **Nicholas Yovanovich**
    Hastings MI
38. **Nicholas Yovanovich**
    Hastings MI
39. **Sheila Forsyth**
    Irvington NJ
40. **Sheila Forsyth**
    Irvington NJ
41. **Karin Bradberry**
    Albuquerque NM
42. **Karin Bradberry**
    Albuquerque NM
43. **Gary McGregor**
    Hattiesburg MS
44. **Graham Kash**
    Cookeville TN
45. **Marilyn Mitchell**
    Laguna Woods CA
46. **Robert Carl Williams**
    Pittsfield VT
47. **Jadene Felina Stevens**
    Harwich MA
48. **Anne Taylor**
    Portland OR
49. **Kathleen McKinley Harris**
    Charlotte VT
50. **Marlene Million**
    Noblesville IN
51. **Robin Clair**
    Lafayette IN
52. **Wayne Lee**
    Santa Fe NM
53. **John F. Bellamy**
    Aurora CO
54. **N. Colwell Snell**
    Salt Lake City UT
55. **Gwendolyn White**
    South Windsor CT
56. **Annabelle Moseley**
    Dix Hills NY
57. **Annabelle Moseley**
    Dix Hills NY
58. **Linda Knowlton Appel**
    West Linn OR
59. **Suzanne Morrone**
    San Jose CA
60. **Paul I. Freet**
    Fayetteville PA
61. **John Carothers**
    Mays Landing NJ
62. **Matthew Wanniski**
    Marina del Rey CA
63. **Kristofer Nivens**
    Grand Rapids MI
64. **Angel S. Krasnegor**
    Charlottesville VA
65. **Nonnie Frenzer**
    Omaha NE
66. **Lisa Parsons**
    Portland OR
67. **Margo Jodyne Dills**
    Seattle WA
68. **R.H. Peat**
    Auburn CA

69. **Nan Hunt**
    Woodland Hills CA
70. **Nan Hunt**
    Woodland Hills CA
71. **Marla Alupoaicei**
    Frisco TX
72. **Jill Suzanne Coleman**
    Hesperia CA
73. **Mary-Alice Boulter**
    Port Angeles WA
74. **Margaret Kerns**
    Washington DC
75. **Gladys L Henderson**
    Nesconset NY
76. **Janice Cutbush**
    Ballston Spa NY
77. **Anne-Marie Legan**
    Herrin IL
78. **Anne-Marie Legan**
    Herrin IL
79. **Anne-Marie Legan**
    Herrin IL
80. **Anne-Marie Legan**
    Herrin IL
81. **Stephen Vincent Miller**
    Laguna Beach CA
82. **Cristine A. Gruber**
    Riverside CA
83. **Marianne Lock**
    Oxford AL
84. **Marianne Lock**
    Oxford AL
85. **Kim Bissett**
    Portland OR
86. **Mary Down**
    Yarmouth ME
87. **Susanna Forrester Hearn**
    Franklin NC
88. **Susanna Forrester Hearn**
    Franklin NC
89. **Linda Simon-Wastila**
    Reisterstown MD
90. **Linda Simon-Wastila**
    Reisterstown MD
91. **Norbe Birosel Boettcher**
    Marion IA
92. **George Meadows III**
    Richmond VA
93. **N. Colwell Snell**
    Salt Lake City UT
94. **Suzanne Morrone**
    San Jose CA
95. **Jose Caraballo**
    San Antonio TX
96. **Nonnie Frenzer**
    Omaha NE
97. **Sienna Elizabeth Raimonde**
    Orchard Park NY
98. **Edward P. Schmidt**
    Blue Ridge GA
99. **J. Graham Ducker**
    Oshawa ON Canada
100. **Sandra Fink**
    Dowling Park FL

RHYMING POETRY WINNERS

1   Annabelle Moseley
    Dix Hills NY
2   Robert Daseler
    Sacramento CA
3   Herb Wahlsteen
    Farmingville NY
4   Marla Alupoaicei
    Frisco TX
5   Robert Daseler
    Sacramento CA
6   Robert Daseler
    Sacramento CA
7   Shirley Windward
    Santa Monica CA
8   Belle Rollins
    Pineville LA
9   Melissa Cannon
    Nashville TN
10 Linda Knowlton Appel
    West Linn OR
11 George (Bud) Stege
    Melbourne FL
12 Soma Mei Sheng Frazier
    San Leandro CA
13 Michelle Perez
    Secaucus NJ
14 James Arthur Anderson
    Miami FL
15 Annabelle Moseley
    Huntington Station NY
16 Annabelle Moseley
    Huntington Station NY
17 Annabelle Moseley
    Huntington Station NY
18 Herb Wahlsteen
    Farmingville NY
19 Herb Wahlsteen
    Farmingville NY
20 Herb Wahlsteen
    Farmingville NY
21 Robert Daseler
    Sacramento CA
22 Robert Daseler
    Sacramento CA
23 Robert Daseler
    Sacramento CA
24 Robert Daseler
    Sacramento CA
25 Robert Daseler
    Sacramento CA
26 James Arthur Anderson
    Miami FL
27 Janet Ireland Trail
    Greensboro NC
28 Melissa Cannon
    Nashville TN
29 Melissa Cannon
    Nashville TN
30 Melissa Cannon
    Nashville TN
31 Melissa Cannon
    Nashville TN
32 Angel S. Krasnegor
    Charlottesville VA
33 Kit Hewes
    Canaan NH
34 Kimberly Sherrell
    Athens TX

35 Marla Alupoaicei
    Frisco TX
36 N. Colwell Snell
    Salt Lake City UT
37 Michelle Perez
    Secaucus NJ
38 Jahnavi-Rose
    Jolireve Laurent
    Jacksonville FL
39 Jahnavi-Rose
    Jolireve Laurent
    Jacksonville FL
40 Jahnavi-Rose
    Jolireve Laurent
    Jacksonville FL
41 Kathleen J. Farrell
    Payson AZ
42 Sharon Gehbauer
    Pearland TX
43 Victoria Rivas
    Waterbury CT
44 Mary Ann Murdoch
    Lakeland FL
45 Mary Ann Murdoch
    Lakeland FL
46 Soma Mei Sheng Frazier
    San Leandro CA
47 Dorothy Lamar
    Woodbury NJ
48 Karin Bradberry
    Albuquerque NM
49 Jack Miles
    Wilmington DE
50 Thomas Fullmer
    Salt Lake City UT
51 N. Colwell Snell
    Salt Lake City UT
52 Faith Ingle Collins
    Sandy TX
53 N. Colwell Snell
    Salt Lake City UT
54 Walter Rein
    Micaville NC
55 Walter Rein
    Micaville NC
56 Del Gustafson
    Duvall WA
57 Cameron Cook
    Chapin SC
58 Angel S. Krasnegor
    Charlottesville VA
59 Angel S. Krasnegor
    Charlottesville VA
60 Angel S. Krasnegor
    Charlottesville VA
61 Del Gustafson
    Duvall WA
62 Amy Stephenson
    Woodbridge VA
63 William Georato
    Salem NH
64 Matthew Legall
    Winnipeg MB Canada
65 Ryan Tilley
    Longwood FL
66 Molly Dee Anderson
    Seattle WA

67 Patrick J. Walker, Jr.
    Factoryville PA
68 Matthew Legall
    Winnipeg MB Canada
69 Kate McGovern
    Newton NJ
70 Amy Chapman
    Greenwood ME
71 Debbie Walker
    Stockbridge GA
72 Soma Mei Sheng Frazier
    San Leandro CA
73 Soma Mei Sheng Frazier
    San Leandro CA
74 Heidi Tompkins
    Chattanooga TN
75 Colleen Carias
    Santa Fe NM
76 Jo Abi
    Castle Hill Australia
77 Katherine Swinehart
    Ferndale MI
78 Karin Gustafson
    New York NY
79 Lisa Arguello
    New York NY
80 Kit Hewes
    Canaan NH
81 Kit Hewes
    Canaan NH
82 Sybil L. Holloway
    Bloomsburg PA
83 Verna Lee Hinegardner
    Hot Springs National Park AR
84 Joyce Dolce
    Pleasant Valley NY
85 Kimberly Sherrell
    Athens TX
86 Ann Robinson
    Sarasota FL
87 Darla Dee Burris
    Alliance OH
88 J. E. Pickens, Jr.
    Owensboro KY
89 Marion Smith
    Ottawa ON Canada
90 Lori White
    Sibley IA
91 Michael F. Albro
    Milford MA
92 James D. Pretkelis
    Saint Charles IL
93 Mary Ann Murdoch
    Lakeland FL
94 Phyllis Turk
    Brooklyn NY
95 Melanie Moen
96 Jerry J. Wilson
    Mason MI
97 Arnot McCallum
    Tecumseh ON Canada
98 Deborah L. Diesen
    Grand Ledge MI
99 N. Colwell Snell
    Salt Lake City UT
100 John Warth
    Seattle WA

STAGE PLAY WINNERS

1 Robert Taylor
  Akron OH
2 Ron Radice
  Andover MA
3 S.R. Anzalone
  Bronx NY
4 Jacob Appel
  Scarsdale NY
5 Scott Openshaw
  Draper UT
6 Jerry Mahoney
  Los Angeles CA
7 Jacob M Appel
  New York NY
8 Jennifer Bogush
  Cranford NJ
9 Barbara Pinsof
  Northbrook IL
10 Nicholas Wardigo
  Ardmore PA
11 Christina J DeSimone
  Brooklyn NY
12 Jessica Crites
  Saint Cloud MN
13 R.W. Swartz
  Wasilla AK
14 Donald Orwald
  Granbury TX
15 M. John Bohane
  Nokomis FL
16 Don Orwald
  Granbury TX
17 George M Johnson
  Kamloops BC Canada
18 Chris Hare
  Moorpark CA
19 Meghan O'Neill
  Brooklyn NY
20 Terrence C Hissong
  Adrian MI
21 Greg LeGault
  Crest Hill IL
22 Lee Kiszonas
  Philadelphia PA
23 Carl L Williams
  Houston TX
24 Christina Hamlett
  Pasadena CA
25 Mana Rokas
  San Francisco CA
26 Leigh Hunt
  Gig Harbor WA
27 Lynne M Smelser
  Brighton MI
28 Matt Tudor
  Fairhaven MA
29 Joe G Hardin Jr.
  Mobile AL
30 Donald Orwald
  Granbury TX
31 Tencha Avila
  Denver CO
32 Roy Robbins
  Cartersville VA
33 Adam Carr
  Staten Island NY
34 Ken Weitzman
  Atlanta GA

35 Roy Haymond
  Centenary SC
36 Kristen Maree Cleary
  Yonkers NY
37 Bill Zettler
  Mundelein IL
38 Peter Broner
  Salt Point NY
39 Michael Reimann
  Orlando FL
40 Amalena Folic Caldwell
  Plantation FL
41 Jennifer Bogush
  Cranford NJ
42 Walter Thinnes
  New York NY
43 Rodney A Nelsestuen
  St. Paul MN
44 Kyla Kordell
  Ewing MO
45 Eric Dawe
  Lansing MI
46 Andrew Hinderaker
  Chicago IL
47 Kim Ben-Porat
  La Jolla CA
48 Kathleen A McLaughlin
  La Mesa CA
49 Michael L Harrington
  Cambridge MA
50 Rene Mrech
  Brownstown MI
51 Aoise Stratford
  Ithaca NY
52 Robert Eagleman
  Alpine CA
53 J.R. Heher
  Kirkland WA
54 J.D. Eames
  Louisville KY
55 Rene Mrech
  Brownstown MI
56 Anne Wycoff
  Lori Kennedy
  San Francisco CA
57 Donald Orwald
  Granbury TX
58 Dan Roth
  North Hollywood CA
59 Brent Englar
  Finksburg MD
60 James Henderson
  Renton WA
61 Donald Orwald
  Granbury TX
62 Jason Boies
  Staten Island NY
63 Jeff Herwig
  Madison WI
64 Jacqueline
  Renee Ahl
  Wallkill NY
65 John Bandler
  Dundas ON Canada
66 James Henderson
  Renton WA
67 Dean Stewart
  Sylmar CA

68 Kent Hinckley
  La Jolla CA
69 Krista K Burlae
  Lincoln NE
70 Donald Orwald
  Granbury TX
71 Fierce Productions, LLC
  Fort Worth TX
72 Dennis Carter
73 Rob Zellers
  Pittsburgh PA
74 Alvin Thomas Ethington
  Claremont CA
75 J.D. Eames
  Louisville KY
76 Jaynie Roberts
  Vancouver WA
77 Cuauhtmoc Q. Kish
  San Diego CA
78 Helen Argers
  Newark NJ
79 Edward Currelley
  Brooklyn NY
80 Carolyn Tippi Young Parmerter
  Rochester NY
81 Donald Orwald
  Granbury TX
82 Marcia R Rudin
  Sanibel FL
83 Jess M Orenduff
  Valdosta GA
84 Kim Brundidge
  Atlanta GA
85 Donald Orwald
  Granbury TX
86 Brian Doohan
  Columbus GA
87 Marcia R Rudin
  Sanibel FL
88 Amanda Minogue
  New Orleans LA
89 Ron Radice
  Andover MA
90 Robert Weesner
  Columbus OH
91 Richard Beck
  Durham NC
92 Gene Descoteau
  St. Augustine Beach FL
93 Maro Kentros
  Seattle WA
94 Scott A Tarapczynski
  Niagara Falls NY
95 Joanna Perry-Folino
  Berkeley CA
96 Madeline Ann Martin
  San Luis Obispo CA
97 Adam Musil
  Austin TX
98 Beverly Little john
99 Jake La Jeunesse
  Houghton MI
100 Joe Molnar
  Brooklyn NY

TELEVISION/MOVIE SCRIPT WINNERS

1 **Charles C. Nwachukwu**
Carrollton TX

2 **Nicolette Vajtay**
Denver CO

3 **Yaphathtoar Colebrooke**
Pasadena CA

4 **Jay Biederman**
Los Angeles CA

5 **K.C. Otenti**
Millville MA

6 **Larry Brenner**
New York NY

7 **David M. Thomas**
Monterey CA

8 **James C. Burau**
White Bear Lake MN

9 **Kim Gerber**
Calabasas CA

10 **Cassandra E.O. Winter**
Portland OR

11 **Ona Lepard**
East Helena MT

12 **Eric Friese**
San Francisco CA

13 **Dean Stewart**
Sylmar CA

14 **Al DeFilippo**
West Palm Beach FL

15 **Harry Wilkinson**

16 **Andrew Jamieson**
Vancouver WA

17 **Joshua Lee**
Iowa City IA

18 **Aaron Clarence Ellis**
Chino CA

19 **Cat Sides**
North Hollywood CA

20 **Brian Trent**
Waterbury CT

21 **Cora Kerr**
El Cajon CA

22 **Steve Duncan**
Los Angeles CA

23 **P.K. Hendrickson**
Rockford IL

24 **Tian Ettevy**
Quincy IL

25 **Janice Spielberger**
San Antonio TX

26 **Jennifer Martin**
Roseville CA

27 **Cat Sides**
North Hollywood CA

28 **Ona Lepard**
East Helena MT

29 **Carol Lee Hall**
Union City CA

30 **Edmund J. Webb**
Coatesville PA

31 **Carol C. Farrand**
San Rafael CA

32 **Christopher M. Acosta**
Bay Saint Louis MS

33 **Janet Russell**
Petaluma CA

34 **Lindbergh Cornell**
Country Club Hills IL

35 **Morgan Saylor Jones**
Portland OR

36 **Donal Harding**
Arden NC

37 **Jett Farrell**

38 **Scott Mercer**
Los Angeles CA

39 **Brian Trent**
Waterbury CT

40 **John J. Smith**
Plano TX

41 **Kathleen Tully**
Kennett Square PA

42 **Teri Short**
Patuxent River MD

43 **John L. Martins, III**
Sierra Vista AZ

44 **Geoffrey Saunders**
Middletown CT

45 **Dion Owens**
Chicago IL

46 **Ami McCuaig**
Seattle WA

47 **La' Chris Jordan**
Seattle WA

48 **Gina Leone**
Farmingville NY

49 **Rebecca J. Herring**
Tustin MI

50 **Julia Detering**
Seattle WA

51 **Bradd Hopkins**
Santa Fe NM

52 **Joe Luca**
Glendale CA

53 **Rick DiMille**
Little Elm TX

54 **Stephanie Dube**
Corpus Christi TX

55 **Tyler Voss**
Fallon NV

56 **C. V. Herst**
Oakland CA

57 **John Lewis**
Dave Coulier
El Segundo CA

58 **Kelley Wilson**
Edmonton AB Canada

59 **Jim Heher**
Kirkland WA

60 **John Stimson**
Van Nuys CA

61 **Diane Murakami**
Honolulu HI

62 **Keith M. Tracy**
Punta Gorda FL

63 **Karma Christine Salvato**
Oak Park CA

64 **Jan Weeks**
Grand Junction CO

65 **Cheryl Rae**
Austin TX

66 **Amanda Hunsucker**
King City MO

67 **Wilson Jackson**
Charlotte NC

68 **Cecil Ronald**
Jamaica NY

69 **B. Jas**
Waterdown ON Canada

70 **Ronald Smith**
Los Angeles CA

71 **Edmund J. Webb**
Coatesville PA

72 **Julie Hairston**
Leesburg VA

73 **Mary Lou Widmer**
New Orleans LA

74 **Ronald L. Boyer**
Santa Barbara CA

75 **Kevin Carmichael**
Millis MA

76 **Michelle Chiacchia**
Buffalo NY

77 **John Mollica**
Cliffside Park NJ

78 **Michelle Chiacchia**
Buffalo NY

79 **Doris B. Gill**
Walnut Creek CA

80 **Stephanie Dube**
Corpus Christi TX

81 **Justine Cowan**
Kensington MD

82 **Kyle Michael Sullivan**
Los Angeles CA

83 **Sarah Billington**

84 **Shane Marquardt**
Nashville TN

85 **David Rech**
Seattle WA

86 **Elizabeth A Stevens**
Lecompton KS

87 **Xylina Rae Kinsey**
North Pole AK

88 **John Stimson**
Van Nuys CA

89 **Elizabeth A. Stevens**
Lecompton KS

90 **Tonha Renee Stidhum**
Chicago IL

91 **Tom Lavagnino**
Los Angeles CA

92 **Lisa Schnell Sottile**
Lebanon OR

93 **John Lewis**
El Segundo CA

94 **Carlene Webb**
Nashville TN

95 **Lesile Choate**
Lawton OK

96 **Sandi Craig**
Glendale CA

97 **Michael D. Zungolo**
Joseph DiSante

98 **Sandi Craig**
Glendale CA

99 **Cecil Ronald**
Jamaica NY

100 **Dahlynn McKowen**
Ken McKowen
Orangevale CA

DISCOVER HOW EASY PUBLISHING YOUR BOOK CAN BE

Available at Amazon.com
for $5.95 or as a free
e-book at
www.OutskirtsPress.com